KILLER'S PHILOSOPHY

She started to get up quickly, clutching her purse. He clamped a hand on her wrist and held it.

"I'm seeing you as a favor to Klegg," Macklin said. "I don't need the work."

"Fine. Because if you think I'm going to pay you to—"

"Kill Blossom. Let's stop waltzing around it. Sit down." His fingers tightened.

Glaring, she obeyed. He withdrew the hand. She rubbed the red spots on the underside of her wrist. "Violence never solves anything."

"It solves almost everything. It's why we arm the police, and it's why we still have wars. Have you ever thought about how many lives would have been saved if some enterprising assassin had stabbed Hitler in that beer hall in Munich?"

Other Peter Macklin thrillers
by Loren D. Estleman

Kill Zone
Any Man's Death

Published by
THE MYSTERIOUS PRESS

ROSES ARE DEAD

LOREN D. ESTLEMAN

THE MYSTERIOUS PRESS • New York

To my brother, Charles

Chapter One

Goldstick thought, here's my partnership.

With the marinated grace of a professional pallbearer, the young attorney held the door for the frumpy woman in the dark skirt and beige silk blouse and drifted past her to slide out the chair on the clients' side of the desk. When she sat down, a small triangle of bare flesh showed at her waist where she'd neglected a button. Wads of Kleenex boiled out of her shoulder bag when it touched the floor. But it was an expensive bag.

From behind the desk he liked what he saw even better. In the puffy face framed by its horseshoe of gray-streaked blond hair he read anger and the ache for revenge. It carried down to her hasty dress and the solid way she sat, as if she were filling a notch in a fort wall. This one wasn't going to go gooey on him at the bargaining table and accept the first offer made by her husband's attorney. It shaped up to be a profitable relationship, one an ambitious young barrister with a Galahad flair could ride to a slot on the company letterhead.

He touched the razor point of a hard pencil to the page of notes his secretary had taken over the telephone. "Your husband's name is Peter Macklin?"

"That's right."

"And you've been married seventeen years?"

"As of last May."

"You have a son named Roger, age sixteen?"

"Seventeen next month."

The next month was November. Goldstick did some mental arithmetic and decided not to press the matter. He was of a generation that was always a little surprised to learn that it had not invented sex before marriage. "You're seeking a divorce on what grounds?"

"Well, the legal terminology is your department. But I'm sick of being married to the son of a bitch."

"Breakdown of marriage," he wrote in the margin of the sheet before him.

"May I ask who recommended us to you?"

"My neighbor, Marge Donahue. You handled both her divorces and she owns a Mercedes."

He loved it. Aloud he said: "The object, of course, is not to make you wealthy, although your support is imperative. We're chiefly interested in seeing that you receive fair compensation for the years you invested in the partnersh— the marriage."

"Mr. Goldstick." She finished lighting a cigarette and spoiled the immaculate brass ashtray on her side of the desk with the burned match. "I'm chiefly interested in taking the bastard for every cent he has. You're chiefly interested in getting your cut. Let's get that straight before we both climb in up to our chins."

He watched her for a moment. She looked like a woman in her forties but was probably younger, given the statistics involving parents of teenaged children. Her eyes were light and pretty in a face going to fat and showing the beginnings of whiskey welts. Take off fifteen pounds, cut back on the chain cocktails; he had seen the transformation take place enough times once the pressure of a bad marriage was released. He asked some more questions, not paying much attention to the answers, letting the rhythm lull them into the conspiratorial atmosphere so crucial to a successful divorce action. There would be plenty of time later for his secretary to get the stuff down.

"What does your husband do for a living, Mrs. Macklin?" he asked.

"He's a killer."

It took him a moment to assimilate the answer. By then he had already written it down. He read it and looked up. "I'm afraid you misunder— Do you mean to say he beats you?" His inner cash register chimed.

"No, I mean he kills people for a living. He's a killer for hire."

He smiled tentatively. Her face didn't move. Smoke curled in front of it. "You're serious?"

"Ask the widows of his victims."

"A hit man."

"A killer."

He nodded, made two marks with the pencil, and sat back, tickling his ear with the eraser. "And what is his gross income?"

Jack Dowd drove into the little lot behind the apartment complex in Southfield, spotted the silver Cougar, and parked two slots down.

He didn't get out of the car. At forty-six, with twenty-two years in the investigation business, he knew better than to accost a subject at his door, on enemy ground with only one way to run when the job was finished. What you did was you followed him to neutral territory and served the papers there. Preferably with a fence to jump over afterward and a supply of witnesses handy, not so much to confirm success as to save yourself a severe beating like the one he had drawn his first week on the job from a Chrysler dock foreman. The court had awarded Dowd twenty-five hundred dollars in damages (someone else had served *those* papers), and he had given no one else the opportunity to be sued by him.

The weather was cooling, but the sunlight refracting through the windshield was drowsily warm. He cranked down the window to avoid succumbing, tilted his porkpie hat forward, and slid a fresh toothpick between his lips from the pocket where he used to keep cigarettes. This had the effect of shooting his jaw and bulldogging his potato-lumpy face. It was how he had posed for the picture he ran with his display in the Yellow Pages.

After two hours the mark came out of the building in jeans and a white knit shirt and got into the Cougar and drove out of the lot. Dowd took a second to compare the man's features with the photograph he'd been given. An ordinary face, a little jagged under a middle-aged quilt of tiredness and worry, hairline creeping back from a sharp widow's peak. The investigator gave the car two blocks, then pulled out behind it.

The Cougar was fast, its driver the kind that seldom misses a light. Dowd had to knock a piece off the red at Eleven Mile Road to keep up. The Cougar cruised along at forty-five for another minute, then made an abrupt lane change and turned into a mall at Twelve Mile. Dowd started to follow. A blue hatchback coming up on his right blatted its horn and he swung back into his lane. He squirted ahead to the intersection, made a right, and came in the back way. Meanwhile he'd lost sight of his quarry.

Prowling the lot, he worried. Getting shaken was nothing. It was the risk you ran when you tailed someone solo, and there were always other chances. But he didn't like thinking that maybe his man had made him. He knew nothing about this one beyond his name, Macklin, and license plate number and that he was self-employed. Usually he insisted on more information, but this particular legal firm paid a healthy retainer for the privilege of playing close to the buttons and Dowd had no wish to work past fifty. Still, the older a man got the more aware he became of the crazies around him.

But when he found the car, parked a quarter mile from the mall entrance with its nose pointed toward the driveway leading out, he stopped worrying and backed into a vacant space across the aisle to wait some more.

The wait was much shorter this time. When Macklin appeared at the head of the aisle carrying a large paper sack in the crook of his arm, Dowd got out and started toward him, eyes on the other end, hurrying his gait a little like a busy man on an errand. Which he was, but not in the way he wanted his subject to think. As they drew near each other, Macklin's gaze flicked over him casually and moved away.

They were almost abreast when Dowd reached two fingers into the inside pocket of his jacket for the summons. Instantly that wrist was seized in an iron grip and he was spun and his own arm was jerked across his throat with his elbow under his chin, and something stiff found his right kidney. He was dimly aware of loose oranges and food cans rolling across the pavement from the sack the man had dropped. Propelled between parked cars by his assailant, he stumbled over one of the items.

A woman in her thirties pushing a cart down the next aisle with a small child in the seat glanced at the two men, then stepped up her pace, staring straight ahead.

"I'm unarmed!" Dowd gasped.

A pause, then the object was withdrawn from his kidney and an empty hand came around in front of him and prowled over his chest and abdomen, paying special attention to the pocket the investigator had been reaching for. It slid inside the jacket and drew out the fold of fine-printed paper. The man's breathing was close to Dowd's ear and he heard the whispered words "dissolution of marriage."

A further search uncovered Dowd's credentials and honorary sheriff's star. Then he was released with a shove. He clawed at the door handle of a battered van to keep from falling. When he turned, Macklin gave him back his badge and ID. Something bulged above the waistband of his jeans under the white shirt.

"Okay, I'm served," he said. "Get out."

There was an unspoken *or* in the speech that the investigator didn't wait around to hear. He adjusted his hat and walked back to his car, leaning forward on the balls of his feet with his shoulders hunched, still feeling the thing that had been prodding his back.

A loud bang shattered the peace of the parking lot and he screamed. Two lanes over, a supermarket bag boy in an orange apron and leatherette bow tie stared at him curiously, then resumed slamming abandoned shopping carts into the train he was pushing. Dowd started moving again. The toothpick he had been chewing was gone. He hoped he hadn't swallowed it.

Getting into the car he thought, Four years to retirement is too long.

Peter Macklin waited until Dowd's car was in the street before looking again at the paper in his hand. He read it all the way through, then refolded it and doubled it and thrust it into his hip pocket. He scowled at the scattered groceries. He hadn't wanted them, had only used the shopping trip as an excuse to lure out the man he had seen watching his car in the lot behind his apartment house.

Something poked him in the stomach when he bent to retrieve the sack. He straightened, pulled the loose green banana out from under his shirt, and dropped it in the sack with the others before attending to the rest of the mess. A man facing divorce couldn't afford to waste food.

Chapter Two

Howard Klegg's office looked like a lawyer's office in an old movie. It was a comfortable old shoe of a room with a dizzying tower of leather-bound books against one wall and a single window looking out on the rough neighborhood, and a big bleached desk with a wing-backed chair behind it, and a sofa and two easy chairs covered in green leather in one corner. Its only luxury, a Persian rug embroidered in gold and silver thread, left the hardwood floor bare for two feet around it.

The lawyer caught Macklin looking at the rug and said, "A gift from a temporarily embarrassed client in lieu of my fee. Times are tight. So far I haven't accepted any chickens or homemade apple pies."

Macklin made himself comfortable in one of the easy chairs and said nothing about Klegg's eight-hundred dollar suit or the ruby studs in his cuffs. Beyond that, and except for his manicure and the expensive cut of his thick white hair, the old man might have been as bad off as he pretended. He was painfully thin, as if he hadn't eaten in weeks. Macklin had had to wait an hour and a half for him to come back from lunch at the Renaissance Club.

Now Klegg walked back and forth the length of the office, carefully avoiding the costly rug as he read over the summons his visitor had handed him. His tongue bulged inside his cheek and Macklin imagined he could see it through the translucent skin.

"It's very much in order, medieval phraseology and all," he said, returning the document. "Why did you come to me? This firm has never handled divorce cases."

"At the moment you're the only lawyer I know. I thought you could recommend someone. For old times' sake," he added.

"You needn't remind me of past services, Macklin. Just because a man is no longer interested in women doesn't mean he's grown senile too."

Macklin didn't think Klegg had lost interest in women either. "How's Maggiore?" he asked.

"Holding his nose against the water rising around him, I suppose. In any case his legal problems are not mine. I never did represent him, just his predecessor. Boniface's case comes up before the parole board next month, incidentally."

"I heard." Nine people had died to arrange the hearing, all by Macklin's hand.

"I saw him yesterday. He wants you to come back to work for him. At a substantial salary adjustment, naturally."

"Tell him thanks."

"The free-lancer's is a precarious existence," Klegg said. "If you thought supporting a wife was tough, wait until you try supporting a divorced one. Boniface can handle that, set up a decoy statement of earnings that would satisfy any court-appointed auditor. It's one of my specialties. And we haven't even discussed the legal protection available in the event of your arrest, which is a danger you can't overlook in your work."

"I just want the name of a good divorce lawyer."

"You don't understand the extent of your former employer's generosity. Quitting is not a word in the jargon of this organization. Your past record is the only reason your case hasn't been disposed of as others have."

"Also Boniface can't afford the loss of manpower."

Klegg lowered membranous eyelids showing a network of

tiny blue veins. Then he raised them, nodded once. "I'll represent you at the divorce hearing."

"I can't touch your fee. I don't own a Persian rug."

"We'll trade services."

Macklin said, "You?"

"No." The lawyer walked back to his desk, wrote something on the top sheet of a yellow legal tablet on the blotter, tore it off, and brought it over. "This is the number of a young woman named Moira King. Her late father, Louis Konigsberg, was my partner. We started this firm together."

"What's she want?"

"She doesn't know. Yet. I do, and when you've heard her out, so will you. One of your jobs will be to convince her of its wisdom."

"I kill people, Mr. Klegg. I don't debate them."

"That's why the trade."

Macklin looked at the sheet in Klegg's hand. He hadn't taken it yet. "My part is just seeing her. Anything else I do I get paid for."

"That's between the two of you."

Macklin read the number, memorized it, and waved away the sheet without touching it. He handled as few objects as possible in unfamiliar places. He liked to keep track of his fingerprints. Standing: "I'll call her. No guarantees."

"None requested." The lawyer was back at his desk, his hand on the telephone-intercom. "I'll have my secretary call this fellow Goldstick, arrange a meeting."

In the hallway outside, Macklin walked past the elevator and opened the red-painted fire door to the stairs. He hadn't taken an elevator in years, not since a colleague of his had been shot full of holes riding one. He never armed himself except when working, preferring to practice evasion over the risk of being caught carrying a concealed weapon. In his business success was measured in birthdays.

He had gone down three steps when a door sighed shut

below and the stairwell echoed with heavy footsteps climbing up. He hesitated, then started backing the way he had come. In this mechanized age he rarely met anyone else using the stairs.

When he was on the landing, a denim-clad black man with a walrus moustache rounded the turn below, clanking as he came. A square backpack affair wrapped in green canvas rode high on his shoulders on a web harness and he cradled a long black tube along his right forearm with a tiny yellow feather of flame wobbling on the end. Their eyes met just as Macklin cleared the entrance and swung the steel door into its frame.

The man on the stairs set his feet and depressed the tube's trigger, trying to beat the closing of the door. A geyser of liquid orange and yellow gushed up the stairs and splattered against the door, blistering the paint and licking back along the fire-resistant walls. The temperature in the stairwell soared. Sweat prickled under the black man's clothes and evaporated as soon as it hit the heated air. He felt as if the oxygen were being sucked from his body and he opened his lips to inhale, charring his lungs with a sudden crackling sear that stopped his heart instantly. His clothes and hair and moustache caught fire and he was still falling when the gasoline in the tank on his back blew, bulging the brick walls beneath the fireproof paneling and shattering every window in the old building.

Klegg's office door sprang open just as Macklin got to it. Except for a quarter-inch horizontal red line on his right cheek that started bleeding while Macklin was looking at it, the lawyer's face was as white as his hair. His eyes flicked behind Macklin to his secretary, getting up from the floor where she had flung herself after the blast, then back to Macklin. "What—"

The killer took Klegg's silk lapels in both fists and rode

him inside. The lawyer's feet went out from under him but
Macklin held him up by the force of their momentum and
Klegg kept going backward until the backs of his legs
touched his desk and he sat down hard on top, ringing the
bell on the telephone. Macklin hung on to his lapels. The
younger man's face was liver-colored.

"I'm set up," he said. "I wonder who."

His tone was dead even. Far away, a fire siren started up,
drawn thin and high through the broken window. Klegg
said, "I don't—"

"Someone who knows I always take the stairs and who
knew when I left this office and called someone."

"Think straight, Macklin. Why would I want you dead?"
Klegg's fingers were spread on the killer's forearms, his thin
wrists jutting like stemware from the loose whiteness of his
cuffs.

" 'Quitting is not a word in the jargon of this organization.' " Macklin mimicked the lawyer's querulous tones.

"In my own building? With a big noise?"

Logic was an attorney's weapon. A fissure showed in the
blank wall before him and he pulled at it with all his train-
ing. "I'm a professional, like you. How do you think I've
lasted this long with my reputation downtown?"

The other held his grip on Klegg's lapels. His face was
unreadable. The lawyer built on his silence.

"Get out of here before the police show up. Call me later."
He told Macklin his home telephone number. "Can you
remember that? After six."

The air was a riot of sirens, the keening of the fire trucks
joined by the deeper bellowing yelp of police cars. Macklin
opened his hands. The lawyer's bunched jacket bore the
imprint of his fists. "It only takes a second to kill you."

"Use the back stairs."

Macklin used the elevator. A lawyer of Klegg's standing
who kept his practice in that neighborhood would be too

cheap to hire *three* killers. He slid into the crowd gathering in front of the building and away.

When the first man in a helmet and raincoat bounded into the foyer, he found threads of black smoke twisting out of the seam around the fire door on that level, carrying with them a sweet smell of roast meat.

Chapter Three

"**M**r. Klegg?"

"Yes."

"My name is George Pontier. I'm an inspector with Detroit Homicide." He snapped his badge folder open and shut with a little turning movement of his wrist.

"Odd, you don't look French."

The black detective grinned appreciatively. He was tall and trim, though not cadaverous like the lawyer, and his soft moustache and gray fringe were barbered to draw the eye down from his bald head to the rough sculpture of his face. His eyes were a startling gray against skin as dark as oiled wood.

"I don't know why they're so down on you at headquarters," he said. "It takes a special kind of person to make that sort of joke knowing how many times I must have heard it."

"Sorry, Inspector. I just got through telling your men for the fifth time what happened here, and it looks like I'm going to have to tell it again."

"Actually, they're not mine. They're with the arson squad. The body makes it my case. But it shouldn't take so long since I'm told you say you don't know what happened."

The corners of Klegg's lips twitched. "You've studied law, Inspector. Don't deny it."

"Two semesters. We didn't get along." He moved his shoulders around under his gray wool suit coat. "Chilly."

"I haven't had time to call a glazier."

Pontier gestured amiably and the lawyer buzzed his secretary and asked her to make the call. Meanwhile the inspector studied the office without moving his eyes. The desk Klegg was standing in front of had been knocked crooked, and some stray pieces of broken glass from the missing window glittered on the floor. The rest would have been driven outward, but one at least had flown inside with enough force to nick the lawyer's cheek, which now wore a fresh pink Band-Aid. Pontier charged the other disarray to the officers who had been tramping in and out for the past two hours. Every place they entered was their place of work and they treated it accordingly.

"You didn't know the dead man?" he asked when Klegg had finished with the intercom.

"I never said that."

"You didn't identify him."

"I was escorted downstairs and shown a charred something in the stairwell. It could have been my brother, if I had one. It could have been barbecued beef or a Chevrolet seat cover. May I ask why I'm being singled out for all this questioning in a building full of witnesses?"

"Top floor's a good place to start. Also you own the building."

"Also?"

"Also you've represented more men with Italian names before grand juries than Campbell has soups and it isn't every day a man pressure-cooks himself to death with a flamethrower in a fireproof stairwell in this city."

"I conduct a legitimate practice according to the ethics of my profession."

"There are easier ways to commit suicide. Someone else was supposed to be standing in front of that nozzle, and if it wasn't you, it was one of your clients."

"That's a broad assumption, Inspector. No wonder you gave up law."

"Your secretary says you came back from lunch about two

o'clock. The blast was reported at two forty-two. What were you doing in the time between?"

"I was in conference."

"That's what she said. She wouldn't say with who."

"She'd be fired if she did. Privilege extends to the entire legal staff."

"Excuse me while I brush all these split hairs off my shoes," Pontier said.

Klegg let his shoulders slump. "I'm an officer of the court, same as you. We both have confidences to keep. We live in a world where anyone who hears voices in his head can arm himself and spray lead into fast-food franchises packed with innocent people. We can't abandon our precepts every time a troubled person cracks."

"Why do I get the feeling you're not going to help me on this?"

"If there are no further questions, I have some more calls to make. You can appreciate what all this has done to my schedule." Klegg circled behind his desk. When he sat down, the detective was leaning on his hands on the other side.

"You're wrong about why I got out of law," he said. "I'm looking at the reason."

Pontier rode the elevator down to the foyer. There the air was thick with wet char and the bitter-metal smell of carbon tetrachloride from spent fire extinguishers. The door to the stairs was propped open, the burned corpse having been removed by men from the medical examiner's office. The inspector spotted a fattish man in a crumpled yellow sport coat standing in a group of officers in uniform. "Lovelady!"

The man wobbled over. He wore his red hair in bangs and his face was a flat white slab with features among the pockmarks. Pontier said, "Trot Howard Klegg through the computer downtown. I want his associates."

"*All* of 'em?" Sergeant Lovelady's voice had been cracking for as long as he had been in the inspector's detail. Pontier had given up waiting for it to finish changing.

"Also I want you to put men on everyone in the building, find out who was seen coming or going between one and three o'clock this afternoon. Get descriptions."

"Jesus."

"I know." The pair left together.

The big man opened the door, looked at the smaller man standing on the flagstones, and rested his thumb outside the lapel of his black suit coat. The smaller man said, "Don't."

Gordy, enormous in black with balloonlike scars over his eyes that eradicated his brows, hesitated. His broken face was incapable of expression. "You carrying?"

Macklin said, "No."

"What you want?"

"See your boss."

"You know what he looks like."

Afternoon sunlight bronzed the surface of Lake St. Clair, visible behind the big Tudor house standing on its square grass island isolated from the rest of suburban Grosse Pointe by an eight-foot wrought-iron fence. Out front a rotating lawn sprinkler swished and pattered on the flagstone walk.

Macklin said, "I can go over you, big as you are."

"I know it."

The lawn sprinkler whispered and pattered. At length a wolfish grin crept over the lower half of Macklin's face, leaving the upper half untouched.

"Whatever he's paying you, Gordy, hit him up for a raise."

"Anything else you want?"

"I still want the first thing."

The big man said nothing.

"Somebody tried to kill me today," Macklin said.

"Surprise."

"In Howard Klegg's building, with a flamethrower."

"It wasn't Mr. Maggiore."

"He confide in you?"

"No, but catering a hit takes time and that's one thing he ain't got much of. He's inside with his accountants. He's been inside with his accountants every day for a month. Trying to stay out of jail. Last thing he's got time for is to have somebody blowed down."

"You forgot. I'm the reason he's inside with his accountants. If Boniface weren't getting out of the box, he'd still be swinging Boniface's clout and IRS wouldn't be smelling blood."

"Yeah, but like I said he ain't had time."

"You're big," Macklin said. "I guess you're as hard as you were when you fought."

"Harder."

"If it gets down to you and me, you'll come off second. You'll hang back when the time comes and I won't. That's the difference."

"I know it."

The tension went out of Macklin's body in a rush. "Hit him up for that raise," he said. "Don't wait."

"He's got other things on his mind."

Gordy was the only man Macklin knew who would put a door in his face. The killer stood there looking at it for a moment. It was one of those times when he was sorry he'd quit smoking. A man with a burning cigarette in his mouth never looked confused. Finally he turned and went back to his car, avoiding the arc of the sprinkler as it came around.

In the sun-filled room Charles Maggiore called the library, the owner of the house looked up from a pile of ledgers and adding-machine tapes on his desk as Gordy entered. Two men wearing blue suits and glasses occupied the chairs on the other side of the desk, one gray-haired, the other barely thirty. They went on checking columns of figures against calculators on the desk as the big man approached.

"Who was it?" Maggiore demanded.

"Peter Macklin."

In the silence following the announcement the gray-haired

accountant looked at Maggiore. All the color had slid from under the blond Sicilian's careful tan.

"What did he want?" he asked.

Gordy told him. The other accountant glanced up, then back to his figures.

"Did you tell him it wasn't me?"

"Yeah."

"He believe you?"

"He ain't here, is he?"

"One of your jobs is to make sure he isn't."

"Yeah."

"Okay." Maggiore returned his attention to the paperwork in front of him.

Gordy left. The gray-haired accountant entered a few more digits into his calculator and said, "You seem relieved."

"I thought it was something else."

Chapter Four

He didn't go home. Familiar places were off limits to the hunted, and Macklin, who had spent at least as much time underground as he had on the surface, held little regard for material possessions he would just have to leave behind the next time things heated up. Thirty-nine years old, a husband—for a while longer, anyway—and a father, and he was no more attached to objects than a kid with his head full of Khalil Gibran.

The nickel-colored Cougar was a target too, but he hung on to it, choosing wheels over feet. He could hot-wire any car made in under three minutes, but an arrest for Grand Theft Auto and a night in the Wayne County Jail would be like strapping himself to the busy end of a shooting range.

Telephone booths too, those few overlooked by Ma Bell in her mania to strip her customers of their last thread of privacy, were forbidden. He cruised downtown Detroit, double-parking and leaving his car in loading zones while he checked out drugstores and diners for open telephone stands in good positions. Finally he found one, at the end of a bar in a cocktail place that commanded a good view of the room and the front door and provided easy exit through the grill. He went back out, parked in a legitimate lot, and used the telephone to call Klegg's home number. Dusk was gathering in clumps outside, and the only illumination in the room came from the rose-colored lights behind the bar.

He was about to hang up when the lawyer answered on the eleventh ring. He sounded breathless.

"You alone?" Macklin asked.

"Yes. Sorry, I was longer than expected getting rid of the police. I just got in."

"They identify the Human Torch?"

"Not yet. They won't for a while. Where are you?"

"Who rigged the kill?"

"I'm not in a position to run it down. I'm seeing Boniface again tomorrow. He'll put it in circulation. Not that he owes you anything now, but he's sentimental."

"I guess we know different Bonifaces."

"Prison has gentled him." Klegg paused. "You still think I set you up?"

"Right now I'm not thinking you didn't. Someone had to know I was there and give the signal when I left."

"I have someone come in and run the place for bugs and wire taps several times a month. The place is clean."

"That doesn't help your case any."

"This morning's electronic miracles are obsolete this afternoon," the lawyer said. "Someone could have been eavesdropping on us through a gun mike from Toledo for all I know. I've been standing up for Boniface and his friends for thirty years, always as an attorney. I don't push buttons on people."

A tall blond waitress in a white blouse and black skirt that caught her just below the pelvis set a tray down on Macklin's end of the bar, gave a drink order to the bartender, and waited while he filled it. Macklin remained silent while her heavily inked eyes slid over him casually.

"Macklin?"

The waitress left with the drinks. "I'm here."

"Are you going to call Moira King?"

He had forgotten all about her. "I haven't thought about it."

"Look, if I were hanging you out to dry I'd find a better

way to do it. I've been in touch with your wife's attorney. My
part of the bargain is started. Call her."

Already the killer was experiencing the frustrations of
working for himself. He had left most of his cash in his
apartment and needed more. He would have to talk to the
woman, even if the job turned out bust.

"I need one thing from you before I set anything up," he
told Klegg.

Klegg asked him what, and he answered. They spoke for a
few minutes more, then Macklin pegged the receiver and
went out through the grill, just in case.

The name Bakersfield said it all.

Accustomed to the damp cool of San Francisco in late
summer, Fred Chao stood inside the steel Quonset on the
outskirts of the minimal town with the appropriate name
and mopped sweat from his neck and wrists with a lawn
handkerchief already soaked transparent. His eyes stung
with salt and he felt greasy in a suit built for the Bay Area
climate. The desert was no place for a middle-aged Chinese-
American businessman. He wondered for the hundredth
time what he was doing sweltering in the only patch of
shade in ten miles of flat, yellow, sun-scorched landscape
when he could be drinking gimlets and enjoying his air-
conditioned view of the Golden Gate Bridge. He had half
decided to get into his rented car and drive back to L.A.
International Airport when the man he had come to see
appeared from behind the red-and-white Aeronca two-
seater parked inside the hangar, wiping his hands off on a
grease-mottled rag.

"Mr. Chow?" The man extended a palm that was not
demonstrably cleaner than it had been before he'd wiped it.

His visitor touched it and withdrew his own quickly.
"Chao."

He could see that the subtle difference in the way he
pronounced the name was lost on his host, who shrugged a

narrow shoulder in a manner peculiarly rural Midwestern. In contrast to the short girth of the Chinese, the other was an inch over six feet and very lean, his coveralls a long narrow sweep of gray cotton smeared black. He had on a cap with OSHKOSH stenciled across the front and a long bill that shadowed most of his face, allowing only his long rectangular jaw to slide out the bottom. It was unshaven and lumped with acne. "My partner says you want Mexico."

"Yes. I want to go to Mazatlán."

"I don't carry dope or nothing like that."

"I just want you to carry me."

"You ain't wanted or nothing like that? That's FBI. Wetbacks is Border Patrol and maybe I pay a fine, lose my license. Leavenworth, that's something else again."

"I'm not wanted. It's perfectly legal. I have a passport."

"You don't need me, then. You could fly Pan Am or drive down. It's a lot cheaper."

"I'd rather not have my name on an official manifest."

The man scratched the lump on his chin, leaving a fresh black smudge.

Chao reached inside his jacket and produced a thick envelope containing ten wilted hundred-dollar bills. "Perhaps this will clear things up."

The man accepted the envelope and thumbed through the contents, wetting the greasy ball twice and moving his lips as he counted. He unzipped a coverall pocket and slid the package inside.

"One suitcase," he said. "Eleven o'clock."

Chao glanced automatically at his wristwatch. It was just three-thirty. "Why so late?"

"I got to finish greasing her, change the oil, clean the plugs. I ain't ate since breakfast. You didn't figure to leave right away."

"What am I supposed to do in the meantime?"

"There's motels in town."

He had seen town. "I'll take my chances in Los Angeles. How do I know you'll be here when I get back?"

"Hell, mister, I own this place. I got more than a thousand bucks in just the building. I'm going to leave it all for one hot night in Tijuana?"

Chao hadn't seen anything he would pay a thousand dollars for since leaving Los Angeles. But he held his tongue and got back into the car. It was too hot to argue.

He decided not to stay in any of the hotels near the airport. If they traced him down here, those would be the first places they'd look. Instead he booked an eighteen-dollar room in a Hollywood motel with an air conditioner that made a lot of noise without shedding much cool air and a TV set that didn't work. He supposed he'd have done as well in Bakersfield, but he felt better in civilization. He double-locked the door and made sure the window was securely fastened, then took off his jacket and tie and shirt and shoes and stretched out on the bed.

But he didn't sleep right away. He thought again of the murder, of the old Chinese man in the underground garage with blood on his silk suit, falling. Of the two younger tailored Orientals turning, the long blade glistening in the one's hand. Of himself running, running and running with his heart slamming his breastbone and running out into the daylight and dodging the honking screeching traffic on the street and running and running, his side cramping, and running and being among people and then slowing down. He thought of the newspaper articles about Tong killings and the grand jury investigation and of going to work and working and going home and sitting and thinking and saying nothing to anyone about what he had seen, and of how safe he had begun to feel again until the police came around asking questions. Then the next morning he opened his front door and saw the Chinese character painted on it in red paint that was still wet. He was second-generation and didn't even know what the sign stood for, but he knew what it meant well enough, and when they killed his dog and left its head on his kitchen table, just let themselves in like there was no lock and left it there for him to find, he called a number on a business card he'd had for a while and here he was in a noisy, airless motel room in Hollywood waiting to catch a plane from Bakersfield to a coastal village in Mexico. Life was funny.

When he looked again it was dark out. He didn't recall having slept. He found the light and read his watch. Eight-thirty. Suddenly he couldn't stand lying down any longer. He turned on the TV and tried to watch a movie, but the picture was full of ghost images and the sound was furred with static. He switched it off and got dressed. He decided to drive around until it was time to go to Bakersfield.

His suitcase was in the car. He inspected his pockets for keys and wallet, felt the lining where he had sewn away another five thousand dollars in hundreds and fifties, turned off the light, and opened the door into the hallway lit only by an exit sign at the near end.

A shadow moved and something struck him where his neck met his shoulder on the right side. There was a flare of sharp, hot pain, then paralysis, but before he could collapse, another blow caught him in the breastbone and he felt it part, like a rotted timber breaking up in deep water. Something struck his head, his stomach, his groin. He fell through the flurry, flung to right and left and back through the open door like a doll in a washing machine. Pain came up in a great curling wave of red and white and broke over his head and took him down into black.

For a full five minutes after his man ceased to move, the young Oriental dressed all in black stood over him, breathing in short, controlled gasps that grew longer and quieter as he stayed motionless. He was small and beardless, his hair worn over his ears and blown into a ledge over his forehead in a shape like a German helmet painted blue-black, disheveled a little by his recent activity. At length he ran his fingers back through it and let the styled layers riffle back down. He was unarmed in the conventional sense; his hands were empty. From behind, his small, fine-boned figure was easily mistaken for a child's. But his black eyes under the Mongolian mantle were ancient, and when at last he moved, turning back into the hall and leaving the door open behind him, it was with a sliding ease that did not look like movement at all.

The car he got into and drove away from the motel lot was stolen. He had chosen it for its nondescript color and style, a vehicle in which to follow a hunted man from Los Angeles to Bakersfield and back without the man noticing. Now he returned it to within a block of where he had taken it and walked three miles back to the house he rented off the Coast Highway.

The telephone was ringing when he let himself in. He walked past it, looked in on his parakeets singing in a cage big enough for a man to stand in before the picture window, tapped some seed from its shaker into the feeder, and folded himself into a hanging basket chair, lifting the receiver on the sixteenth ring.

"Yes." His voice was boyish.

"Detroit calling Chih Ming Shang," announced a female operator.

He corrected her pronunciation of his name and told her to put the call through. The parakeets sang.

Chapter Five

The house stood on a dead-end street in Taylor, a frame building older than its neighbors but better kept, narrow, with a high peaked roof and a rectangular tongue of lawn out front bordered with whitewashed stones to discourage motorcyclists from cutting across it. Macklin left his car on the street and mounted the square concrete stoop to rap on the door. There was a door bell, but people who used it were not welcome, and their rings were not answered.

Floorboards shifted inside and were silent, and Macklin knew he was being observed through the peephole in the center panel. Then a series of locks snapped and a chain jingled and the door opened wide. "Mac. Jesus, get inside."

He obeyed. The door closed and his host flipped all the locks back in place with a single downward stroke of one index finger like a pianist riffling the keys. Blue metal flashed and vanished into a pocket. The hand came back out empty. "You got guts coming here. Don't you know you're glowing?"

"What've you heard?"

"I heard somebody tried to fricassee your ass in Howard Klegg's building yesterday."

"You hear a lot for a man that never goes out."

"You stay put, keep your ears unstopped, people come and tell you things."

They moved through a square arch into a small living room bathed in morning light. Macklin's host was a short man with a cylindrical body sheathed in a white shirt and green work pants with a small square bulge where the gun rested in his right side pocket. He wore his brittle black hair in a tall brush flecked with gray, lengthening a face already shoe-shaped, with tired eyes and a wide mouth and a nose that was divided in the center like buttocks. His skin was naturally brown, though he was Caucasian and almost never went out into the sun. He smelled faintly of lubricating oil.

"Figured you'd know better than to go to a place you been before," he said.

"I need a gun, Treat. You're the only runner I've used more than once in five years and that's as close to trusting someone as I get."

"I deal to Maggiore. If his name's on this one I can't deal to you. It ain't ethics. I like my balls where they are."

"It isn't Maggiore."

"You could just be saying that."

"I could kill you and take the gun."

"You only kill when someone pays you."

"Don't count on it, Treat."

"Tough, tough, *tough*. Come on."

The little man led him down a hallway to the rear of the house, which went back for twice its length to a steep staircase just inside the door of a bedroom scarcely big enough for the bed and the staircase and started up that. "Watch your head."

Macklin did, bending almost double to clear the edge of an open trap that Treat had gone through with a bare nod of his own head. From the opening a length of naked floor stretched between sharply sloping plaster walls that met overhead, papered over with figured ballistics charts and a diagram of an antitank weapon stamped U.S. ARMY ORDNANCE TOP SECRET. A row of rifles and shotguns lined the left wall in racks, wrapped in transparent fiberglass clouded with pink cosmoline. A window in the far wall facing the street had been bricked in and paneled over, and that wall was dotted with felt-covered pegs on which rested a variety of hand-guns. Pieces of a disassembled machine pistol littered a stone-topped workbench against the right wall.

"Schmeisser," said Treat, indicating the components. "Piece of shit compared with what's come out of Middle Europe since the war. But I got two cases of them in a trade with a Bolivian dealer and I figure I can lay them off on some survivalists I know down in North Carolina." He sat down on a wooden bleacher seat and unlocked a drawer in the bench with a key attached to a steel case on his belt.

"No flamethrowers?"

"No. Shit, no. You get into that military shit, get Intelligence on your ass on top of ATF, and you're looking down twenty to life up in Milan. I didn't arm your shooter."

"Maybe you knew him." Macklin described the man in the stairwell.

Treat, rummaging through the deep drawer, shook his head. "He wasn't local, or if he was he was new. I know all the ones worth knowing. Here's what you need." He lifted the pasteboard lid off a white Styrofoam block, removed a square pistol from the cutout, and handed it to Macklin.

The killer turned the gun over in his hands. It was bright nickel steel from butt to barrel, seemingly all of a piece and seven inches long. He found the release catch and the maga-zine slithered out the bottom of the handle. It was empty. He slid it back in. "Nine-millimeter?"

"Ten."

"There's no such thing as a ten-millimeter."

"It's brand-new. The army's going to use it to replace the old Colt forty-five auto."

"I haven't heard anything about that."

"Neither has the army. But it's going to happen. It takes as much punishment as the Army Colt, but it's lighter and packs more wallop. Even the lady dogfaces get to make like Audie Murphy."

"What about ammunition?"

"I can let you have a case for cost."

Macklin gave it back. "I don't like automatics."

"There's no arguing with a brontosaurus," Treat said. "Look over that junk on the wall."

He skimmed the rows of weapons and selected a Smith & Wesson .38 revolver with a fat flesh-colored grip. His fingers molded themselves around the soft rubber. "Feels like flesh."

"Natural rubber. I can put a different grip on it if you want."

"No, I like this one."

"There's lots better guns than the Police Special."

"Not for me. How much?"

"Six."

Macklin looked at him. "It was three last time."

"Last time you were connected. I'm going to start dealing to indies I got to charge according to risk. You say it's not Maggiore who's got the paper out on you. Okay, say you're right. Maybe it's someone else I deal to. I ain't just jumping at shadows. You think I was born with this nose?"

"I've always been curious about that."

"Don't be. Met one shotgun butt, met them all. You got one hell of a nerve, haggling with a man you were threatening to kill ten minutes ago."

"I could still do it and save the six hundred."

"You won't, though."

"Because we're friends?"

Treat rested an elbow on his workbench. "I guess you can't call us that. We never been to each other's place for dinner. I don't even know if you got a wife or kids or if you bowl Tuesdays. But if you run around knocking down people that ain't your enemies, guess what's left."

"At these prices it's hard to tell the difference."

"Hey, I don't have to sell you a gun. There's plenty of runners wouldn't. I'm starting to hack up a doubt or two myself."

Macklin thumbed bills out of the emergency fund in his wallet. "All I've got is five hundred."

"Hang the gun back up."

He stood holding the gun. He never fondled them. "Maybe next time *you're* up to your ass in enemies, you'll remember this moment."

"Hey, I'm touched." Treat fell silent, rubbing the cleft in his nose with the edge of an oil-stained thumb. Macklin wondered if that was really what had happened, years and years of rubbing it with his thumb. "Okay. But you score your own ammunition."

The money changed hands. Macklin kicked out the revolver's cylinder, letting light through the chambers, and snapped it back. "Holster?"

"Jesus Christ." Treat flipped him a scuffed stiff black leather belt clip from the drawer.

Macklin snugged the .38 into it and clipped it on under his shirt inside his pants. He let Treat see his wolf's grin. "You're really not afraid of me, are you? How come?"

"I'm afraid of all the usual things and a couple more. But you work with tigers, you don't let them see you back up. Use the back door, okay? I got a kid coming in for a trumpet lesson at ten."

He'd forgotten Treat taught music as a cover for his upstairs operation. "Okay, thanks."

"Have a nice day."

"Marines on three, George," Sergeant Lovelady reported. "A Lieutenant Wilmot in Enlisted Personnel."

"Take it, will you?" Inspector Pontier was reading through the John Doe autopsy report spread out on his desk. Death due to thermal trauma.

"I think you want to hear this direct."

Pontier looked up at the other's dimpled slab of a face, like a melted golf ball. He took off his reading glasses and lifted the receiver and punched 3. He listened for a few minutes, occasionally inserting a brief question. He thanked the caller and hung up. Lovelady was still in the office.

"One for you," he told the sergeant. "Checking out the military first was an okay idea. Stiff's dental chart kicked out Corporal Keith Alan DeLong, Marine Reserve, three years in West Germany, one week apiece in Beirut and Grenada. Qualified on .45 auto pistol, M-1, M-16 assault rifle, BAR, bazooka—"

"Flamethrower?"

"Also tripod machine gun and antitank weapons. He seems to have had trouble communicating. Negro male, twenty-eight. Last known occupation, construction worker. Last known address, 1809 Livernois, Detroit, apartment 36. Get someone over there." He tore the page of notes off his pad and handed it to Lovelady. "Feed him into the machine and Telex Washington. Anything on the cigarette lighter?"

The other shook his head. "Serial number burned off. No recent break-ins reported at any of the Guard armories in the state. Hell, you can buy the things surplus from any licensed dealer, not to mention any runner who can go the rent on a warehouse."

"Flamethrowers, Christ. What's wrong with a Saturday-night special?"

The telephone burred. Pontier speared it and waved at Lovelady, who went out, drawing the door shut behind him. The deputy chief was on the line.

"You still running down that arson thing?" Piped-in music floated in the background.

"It's not just arson now, Chief. It's starting to look like a professional hit that backfired, excuse the expression."

"If he killed himself it isn't homicide, technically. Nor even attempted, without someone to sign a complaint. You're backed up, George. Kick it back to Arson and move on."

"Give me a week, can you? My guts are grinding on this

one. Howard Klegg's in up to his sheepskin. You know how long he's been stuck in our side."

"Howard Klegg?

Christ, thought Pontier, and explained who Howard Klegg was.

Music played. "Can you ring in organized crime? The mayor likes organized crime. The president hates it and it means millions in federal allocations."

"If I'm right about Klegg being involved I won't have to do any ringing."

"One week. You get anything solid let me know. The chief will want to call a press conference. You'll take part, of course."

Press you, Pontier thought.

After the deputy chief broke the connection, Pontier buzzed Lovelady's desk. "I forgot to ask," he said when the sergeant answered. "What've you got on Klegg's associates and those eyewitness descriptions?"

"Couple of matches and three maybes. I'm waiting on the FBI for the rest."

"Light a fire under them, can't you?"

"What's the hurry?"

"Politicians," spat the inspector. "They've all got watches that run ahead of their brains."

"They got brains?"

Pontier told him to get to work. He returned to the autopsy report, caught himself humming the tune he had heard playing in the deputy chief's office, and stopped. He hated canned music more than he hated politicians and Mob lawyers.

Chapter Six

Brown was appalled at the Oriental's lack of size. "Why, he's just a boy!"

"He's thirty-seven," said the other spectator.

They watched the two men on the mat bowing to each other. The Oriental, half his opponent's size in a white pajama outfit knotted with a plain cord, appeared impatient with the polite opening ceremony. When it was finished and the other man started to circle he launched himself from a standstill, arching his back and driving a pointed bare foot at the end of a straight leg at the man's solar plexus. His opponent dodged late but quickly, catching a glancing blow under his right arm. He spun and lashed out but kicked only empty air as the smaller man ducked, driving in low with his arm stiff. Again he missed the pressure point but drew a satisfying grunt as his bent knuckles found the larger man's ribs.

For a while they circled each other, feinting and drawing back. Then the larger man moved, pivoting on the ball of his left foot and swinging the right high at his opponent's head. Instead of ducking, the Oriental snatched the flying ankle and pulled, at the same time stepping in and hooking a leg behind his opponent's stationary one. Falling, the man twisted to put his hands under him. But the smaller man straightened him with a stiff backhand swipe across his midsection and, in a series of moves too fast for the pair watching to follow, scissored at him with hands and feet until the man lay in a heap on the mat, his chest pumping. The Oriental turned away. Hissing like a reptile, the man on the floor sprang to his feet and threw himself at his opponent's back. The other spun suddenly and jabbed straight out at shoulder level and the hiss turned into a loud croak and the larger man folded up and lay on the mat, rolling from side to side with his hands clutching his throat and his mouth open wide and making no sound.

"Call the paramedics," Brown said calmly.

His companion hurried off to comply. The gymnasium was large and high-ceilinged, with natural light sifting through frosted panels and glimmering on the varnished floor beyond the edges of the mat. Without looking back at his beaten foe the Oriental crossed noiselessly through a door into the locker room. Brown followed him inside without pausing to knock. He was a broad man but not fat, built like a professional wrestler with shoulders that strained the material of a suit that otherwise hung on him like sacking. His square face was doughy-pale, divided exactly in half by a line of blue beard and topped by thick dark graying hair that he combed back with his fingers. His eyes were cod-colored.

"Mr. Shang?"

Naked before an open locker, stuffing his white outfit into a leather gym bag, the Oriental said nothing. He looked even younger without clothes. He was smooth all over, not muscular, and had no hair on his body. His penis was no larger than a boy's. He zipped shut the bag and turned to the clothes in the locker, paying no attention to his visitor.

"The showers here are excellent," Brown tried. "The pressure could pin a man to the floor."

"I didn't work up a sweat."

"Yes, I saw. Did you have to be so rough? Kung Fu sparrers are expensive and hard to come by in this part of the country, unlike California. We'll have to pay him a bonus on top of his hospital bill to keep him from running to the authorities. If he survives."

"I don't work for Occidentals."

He had a slight singsong accent, miles removed from the broad man's lathed-down, carefully cultured American euphony. He buttoned a blue dress shirt and stepped into black wool slacks. He wore no underclothes.

Brown said, "Then may I ask why you accepted our invitation to fly here?"

"I'd never been to Detroit."

"Sure it wasn't something else?"

Shang slammed shut the locker and turned, holding patent leather loafers. "Your name is what?"

"You can call me Mr. Brown."

"Not Smith?"

"For now I like Brown. Chih Ming Shang." He pronounced the name correctly. "I understand a little Mandarin. The name means 'deadly wound,' doesn't it?"

Shang slipped the loafers on over his naked feet and straightened, saying nothing.

"You came because Michigan offers anonymity," Brown suggested. "Your growing reputation has begun to hobble you on the West Coast. Once you've acquired a nickname, your effectiveness is cut in half. The Tongs call you the Shadow Dragon."

"The Tong is an Occidental invention."

"And the Mafia and the KGB are the creations of popular novels and the Sunday comics. But the organizations that bear those misnomers exist. By now you know we didn't bring you here to see this building—which, by the way, I own through a string of dummy corporations that would take Antitrust the next two presidential administrations to sort out. We want you to remove a problem. If you do well we may retain you permanently."

"I'm a martial arts instructor."

Brown laughed softly, spreading his coat.

"I'm not wired. The room isn't bugged. If I were a police officer, I think you'd agree that flying you two-thirds of the way across the continent to trick a confession out of you would fall under gross entrapment."

"Now that I know what you aren't." He let it dangle.

"I'm a government bureaucrat."

"Which government?"

"Do I detect a streak of Chinese-American patriotism, Mr. Shang?"

"I'm half Japanese. My parents spent World War Two behind barbed wire at Manzanar because their eyes slanted. What do you think, Mr. Brown?"

"A good answer. Have you visited your bank lately?"

"Why?"

"I'll take that as a no. If you had, you'd know that at four o'clock yesterday afternoon, Pacific time, the sum of two thousand dollars was deposited in your account. An additional deposit will be made later. Say, five thousand total?"

"I don't do political assassination."

"Just a moment ago you didn't work for Occidentals," Brown mused. "No, this man is quite anonymous, or at least no better known to the general public than you."

"A professional?"

"A user of weapons."

"Guns?"

"Usually. He has a curious superstition, however. He never arms himself unless he's working. At the moment he isn't."

"I can handle a man with a gun. But I have to know he has one."

"He won't if he follows his usual pattern. Can I take it you're hiring on?"

"Why me?" Shang asked. "There are more locals working here than in L.A. and San Francisco combined."

"We tried one. He didn't work out. He was semipro at best. The man who made that mistake is on his way home. I'm his replacement."

"You have a workup?"

"Workup?"

"A report. Description. Habits. Perversions."

"It's waiting for you at your hotel. It's quite thorough. We bought it from one of our underworld contacts with your same realistic approach toward nationalism."

"There's a difference. I'm not a traitor."

"You're a martial arts instructor."

Shang didn't smile. His masklike face looked like the illustrations of Oriental villains on the covers of the smuggled pulp magazines that Brown had read as a boy. *The slitlike eyes of Wu Fang.* "When can you start?"

"After I've read the workup. And called my bank."

Brown showed him a way out of the locker room and the building that wouldn't take him past the ambulance attendants on their way inside to tend to Shang's vanquished opponent. He'd been hearing the sirens coming for minutes. Carrying his gym bag, the small man moved with fluid grace down the narrow alley and around the corner. Brown was glad to see the last of him for a while. Killers had no sense of humor and he never enjoyed working with them.

Chapter Seven

The bar was a green-painted concrete building with a gravel parking lot on a corner across the street and down the block from the General Motors assembly plant in Westland. The lot was deserted, and when the woman entered and her eyes adjusted to the medium light inside she saw no one but a white-haired bartender dozing while standing up in front of the beer taps. She glanced down at her watch, stood there a moment longer, and was about to turn and walk out when a man rose from the other side of the jukebox and beckoned her over.

By the time she got there, he was seated again. The table was narrow, barely large enough to support two drinks, with a hard chair on either end. She said, "I'm Moira King. Are you the man who called?"

"Yes."

"Could we move to a booth? I'd feel more comfortable."

"Booths are too hard to get out of."

When he said nothing more she sat down opposite him, resting her purse on her lap. She was twenty-three but looked much older, her face anorexic-looking with the bones prominent and her eyes large and bright as from fever. She wore her auburn hair short and combed behind ears with amber buttons in the lobes. Her dress was a plain brown shift through which the straps of her white brassiere showed. She dug a cigarette out of her purse and let it droop from the center of her mouth with her thumb poised on the wheel of a disposable butane lighter.

"You didn't give me your name," she said, and lit it.

"You're Louis Konigsberg's daughter."

"Yes." She blew smoke away from the table. "I had my name legally changed. I was going to be an actress for a while. Now I make recordings for the telephone company. When you call for the time? That's me." She closed her mouth before she could run on further. The man's tired-looking eyes seemed to see through her skull. She wondered if he was a policeman.

"Klegg said you had a problem. He didn't tell me what it was."

She puffed at the cigarette, flipped ash into the tin tray on the table, puffed again. She never inhaled. "Can I get a drink? Whiskey sour."

He went on looking at her, then got up and walked over to the bar, rapping a knuckle on the top to wake the bartender. He returned carrying only one glass, which he set in front of her.

"Aren't you drinking?"

"Not when I'm working."

He was a policeman. She sipped her whiskey and set it down. "I don't see how you can help me. The other police said there was nothing they could do until Roy committed a crime."

"Who's Roy?"

"He was my boyfriend. He thinks he still is, that's the problem." She looked around at the empty tables. "I don't see how this place stays in business."

"The shift at the assembly plant doesn't change for two more hours. Then the place is jammed. That's why I picked this time. What's Roy's last name?"

"Blossom. We—made some films together in Detroit two years ago, before I found out I wasn't going to cost Faye Dunaway any sleep. We saw each other off the set. He was good-looking, about twenty-five, tall and blond and fantastic in bed. The joke around the studio was that when the lights went up so did he." She got a sour smile on her face. It wasn't returned. She sent some more ash at the tray. "Then he got arrested."

"Pornography?"

"Murder. He got in an argument with a man in a parking lot over a scratched fender and cut him up with a pocketknife."

"What'd he get?"

"The jury found him innocent by reason of insanity and he went to the forensic psychiatry center at Ypsilanti for sixteen months. They let him out five weeks ago. He called me the day he got out. He's called almost every day since.

"I told him I didn't want anything more to do with him. I said I had a good job and I was happy with my life and I didn't want to go back. I told him it had nothing to do with what he did. It did, of course, but I wasn't going to tell him that."

"He didn't take it well."

She looked at him quickly. His expression hadn't changed. "He said I'd be sorry."

"He say how?"

"He's too smart for that. He calls me at all hours. I changed my number to an unlisted one, but he found it out somehow. I'm afraid to answer the phone. But the ringing and ringing is almost as bad as listening to him. He never says anything specific, just talks about what he's been doing and how he thinks about me all the time. Hell, I can't even get him for making obscene calls. If they were they wouldn't be so bad. It's what he doesn't say. Then last Monday I saw him."

The bartender cruised past, stopping to wipe off a table nearby. She waited until he moved away.

"It was on the sidewalk in front of my apartment building. I was coming home from work and there he was. He was thinner than I remembered and his hair was shorter, but the time in the hospital didn't seem to have hurt him physically. He had a knife with him.''

"He threaten you with it?"

"Yes. Well, not really. He didn't wave it at me or even mention it. He just cleaned his fingernails with it. All the time he was talking he was cleaning his fingernails. It was one of those fancy ones with a lot of attachments. We used to call them Swiss Army knives.''

"What'd he say?"

"Nothing. He just said it was good to see me and that I looked good, said he was job-hunting; small talk. He pretended we met by accident. But he was waiting for me. He offered to see me to the door of my apartment. I said that wouldn't be necessary and he didn't push it. I don't think we were talking for more than five minutes. But all the time he was cleaning his nails with that big knife.''

"Anything else?"

"I think he's been following me. I never see him doing it. I just feel him. He means to kill me, and you people won't do anything to stop him. He was declared sane by psychiatrists, but he's just as crazy as he was when he went to the hospital, and he's going to cut me up just like that man in the parking lot and no one's going to stop him.''

She had raised her voice. The bartender was watching them from across the room. The man stared at him until he looked away. Quietly the man said, "I'm not with the police.''

"You're not? But, Uncle Howard said—"

"He didn't say I was a cop. How much do you know about the law practice he shared with your father?"

She crushed out her cigarette and sat back. "I'm not naive. I've known what kind of clients they represented since I was seventeen.''

"That would be about the time you got into movie-making?"

"About then, yes."

"I used to work for one of their clients," he said. "Michael Boniface."

"Oh." She played with her glass. "A leg-breaker. Well, you won't scare Roy. They had some parts left over when they built him, and the ability to be scared was one of them. If you're the best Uncle Howard could do—"

"I don't scare people. Not for a living. I come in when the leg-breakers give up."

His eyes were on hers. He watched the color subside from her face. She started to get up quickly, clutching her purse. He clamped a hand on her wrist and held it.

"I'm seeing you as a favor to Klegg," he said. "I don't need the work."

"Fine. Because if you think I'm going to pay you to—"

"Kill Blossom. Let's stop waltzing around it. Sit down." His fingers tightened.

Glaring, she obeyed. He withdrew the hand. She rubbed the red spots on the underside of her wrist. "Violence never solves anything."

"It solves almost everything. It's why we arm the police, and it's why we still have wars. Have you ever thought how many lives would have been saved if some enterprising assassin had stabbed Hitler in that beer hall in Munich?"

"That would have been sinking to his level."

"There's only one level, Miss King. It belongs to the survivors."

"I'm not a killer."

"That's why you need me."

She finished her drink and lit another cigarette, looking at him through the smoke.

"I don't even know you're what you say you are. Maybe you're just some grifter who'll take my money and go and I'll still have Roy to deal with."

"My name is Macklin."

A vertical line cracked her forehead.

"I'm sorry you recognize the name," he said. "It's not good to be known outside the business."

She said, "The Boblo boat last summer. Those terrorists."

"My part in it hit the papers for one edition. One of them reported my name. Just once, though. Boniface cuts a wide swath in this area, the FBI too."

"Isn't this out of your line? I mean, individual."

"I'm working for myself these days."

She was silent for a little. Then: "I don't want you, Mr. Macklin. I'm no one to judge what anyone else does for a living. But it was tough getting out and I'm not going back."

"That what you told Roy?"

"I'm sorry. This was a mistake." She started to get up again.

He drew a long fold of paper from inside his jacket, glanced at it to make sure it was the right one, and reached it across the table. She hesitated, then took it and unfolded it. "What's this?"

"In case you change your mind. It's a power-of-attorney form giving me title to everything you own. It's my standard fee."

"Isn't it a bit stiff?"

"It's worth it. If he kills you, you won't need it, and if he doesn't, I'm not necessary. I had Howard Klegg draw it up. That's his secretary's signature in the witness blank. All you have to do is sign it. This too." He handed her another document. "It's a formal confession that you've hired me to commit murder. Spreads the risk a little more evenly."

"You don't take any chances."

"I got out of the habit. There's a post office box number on the confession if you decide to go with me. Sign and mail both papers and I'll get back to you."

She started to give them back. He didn't take them.

"Hang on to them at least until you hear from Blossom again," he said. "You can always burn them. Next time the phone rings maybe you'll remember this moment."

"I won't change my mind." But she put the papers in her purse. She rose and looked down at him. "I'm curious."

"You get one question."

"When the census-taker knocks on your door and asks what you do for a living, what do you tell him?"

"Human relations consultant," he said. "I'll look for your letter."

The white-haired bartender leaning on the beer taps didn't stir as she went past.

Shadows were stretching when Macklin left the bar twenty minutes behind the woman, as was his habit. He had parked his car around the corner on a meterless residential side street. It was the only vehicle in sight at that time of day. With the end of the recession in the automotive industry, the GM assembly plant was running at white heat and everyone seemed to be working.

Before opening the door he routinely inspected the interior through the windows and ran the hood and doors for unfamiliar wires, finally checking the engine and getting down in push-up position to peer under the car. He was climbing to his feet when the man came at him.

He had been crouching behind a hedge in the front yard of the house across the street, and but for the scrape of one sole on the pavement he made no noise coming across, touching ground only once in a whirling bounce, all arms and legs and flying black hair, a tubular body dressed all in black and a flash of ivory face screwed into a grimace of concentration. A pointed foot at the end of a gracefully arched leg streaked toward Macklin's head and he squeaked the Smith & Wesson out of the holster in the small of his back and fired twice into the flying form.

The foot grazed his shoulder and the man on the end of it piled yelling into the side of Macklin's car and dropped in a tangle to the pavement. Macklin put the gun to the man's temple.

The man was still grimacing, his eyes glittering in their slits. "They said," he whispered.

"Who said?" Macklin pulled back the hammer.

"They said you wouldn't—" Blood came into his mouth, choking him. He coughed, and then he stopped coughing.

Macklin lowered the hammer gently as the hate-face relaxed, freed from the burden of a soul. The body arched and settled.

A dog started barking. Putting away the revolver, Macklin patted the body down swiftly. The clothes had no pockets. He got into the car, started the engine, and backed up to drive around the dead Oriental in the street.

The next morning he found a thick envelope addressed to him in his post office box.

Chapter Eight

"**C**ouldn't you have worn a suit?" Howard Klegg scowled at Macklin's brown-and-tan checked sport coat. The lawyer himself was wearing a gray three-piece with a silver stripe.

"It's in my apartment," said Macklin. "I've been living out of motels for two days. I just bought this. It's the only thing I could find that hides a gun."

"You're *armed*? Here?" Klegg swept a long arm around the lobby of the Old County Building. A circuit court judge Macklin recognized from television interviews was showing the sailing-ship mosaic on the floor to a visitor.

"Someone tried me again yesterday. Stairwells aren't good enough anymore. It's public streets now, in broad daylight. Why not a government building?"

"Well, let's just hope you don't bump into a bailiff on the way."

They mounted a broad balustraded staircase. "You talked to Boniface?" Macklin asked.

"Twice since you and I last talked. He drew a blank with his people on why you're marked and who marked you. So far as the street talent in Detroit is concerned, there is no Macklin contract."

"Tell that to the charbroiled stiff and the Chink in the morgue."

"The police identified the man in the stairwell, an unemployed construction worker and ex-Marine named Keith DeLong. No known criminal record."

"Ask higher," Macklin said.

"You ask higher. I've enough to do with this divorce and repairing the damage to my building. My insurance doesn't cover flamethrower explosions."

"Sell the Persian rug."

They had entered pedestrian traffic on the second floor. Klegg held his retort and rearranged his face into the expression he reserved for judges' chambers.

The judge's name was Flutter, and Macklin thought he had never met a man whose name fit him less well. He was a pyramid of pale flesh poured into expensive tweeds and propped between the arms of a chair on a heavy steel frame behind a big desk. His hair was carrot-colored and his cheeks had a white consistency that looked as if they would hold the indentation of a finger minutes after it was withdrawn. Macklin's wife Donna occupied another chair, next to a young man with short black hair permed into glossy waves like corrugated steel and spaniel eyes in a face that came to a point at his chin. He got up to shake Klegg's hand and introduced himself as Gerald Goldstick, and there were more introductions while Macklin kept his hands to himself. In 1924, Dion O'Bannion, crime lord of Chicago's North Side, had offered his hand to a visitor in his flower shop and had it held while another man pumped six bullets into him.

It was a brief meeting, the sides feeling each other out under the somnolent eye of the fat judge seated behind his desk with his fingers lined up like frankfurters on the near edge. Even when the two lawyers were conversing, Macklin felt Goldstick's eyes on him. The young lawyer had a big ruby knot snugged up under his pointed chin and he was forever pulling at it and shooting his cuffs and fingering the spray of handkerchief in his display pocket like a small boy playing dress-up. Macklin supposed Donna had been telling him stories. He wondered if they'd slept together yet.

She looked better than he'd seen her in some time, but then he'd forgotten what she looked like out of the ratty old robe she wore around the house with cigarette burns on the front and drink stains on both sleeves. She had on a neat russet slack suit and cordovan boots and she'd been streaking her hair to disarm the gray, but she hadn't lost any weight and her lipstick was on crooked. He glanced again at Goldstick and decided he'd been wrong about the two of them. The lawyer could do better.

Sparks flew just once, when Klegg submitted Macklin's estimate of his current worth. Donna remained silent while it was being read, then said, "What about the hundred thousand?"

Macklin met her glare. "What hundred thousand?"

"The hundred thousand you got for killing those people on the Boblo boat. I hear things. Even your friends in the Sicilian Sewing League couldn't keep the lid down on that one."

Judge Flutter appeared to waken. The viscous eyes in the yeasty face blinked slowly at her, then at Macklin. "What's this about killing?"

"Figure of speech, your honor." Klegg was looking at Goldstick. "By surrendering this financial statement at this time, my client has more than fulfilled his obligations so early in the action. His investments and savings accounts are all listed here. You're welcome to go looking for secret caches."

"Fuck investments and savings accounts."

"*Mrs.* Macklin." The judge tapped a thick finger like a gavel.

"You don't invest blood money. IRS would want to know where it came from. Under the laws of the State of Michigan I'm entitled to half of that hundred thousand."

"Comment, counselor?" asked Goldstick.

Klegg was busy rearranging papers in his brown leather briefcase. "Mind you, I'm not saying there is any such sum. But if there were, my client's Fifth Amendment rights would shield him from having to declare it."

Goldstick said, "Funny, Al Capone's attorney didn't try that."

"Your precedents are rusty, counselor. Under a 1966 Supreme Court decision involving a number of bookmakers tried for evasion of taxes, immunity from self-incrimination applies to declaring illegal income. This is not to say, of course, that any such income exists in this case."

"Kid games," said Donna, setting fire to a cigarette in the corner of her mouth. "Shit."

The judge drummed his finger.

"Gentlemen, I have seldom seen a divorce action or its answer so ill prepared before court. I suggest you meet on your own and discuss this matter of the hundred thousand dollars and then come back here with smiling faces all in a row. We adjourn for now."

A rabbit warren of offices in a short corridor led to the main hallway. On their way down it Klegg leaned close to his client and whispered: "By the way, what *did* you do with the money?"

"I buried it."

"You're joking."

Macklin looked at him flatly. The lawyer smoothed his tie.

"I forgot. You don't have a sense of humor." They started downstairs. "Call me later. We've got to work out this thing."

"What about the Fifth Amendment?"

"No one listens to the Supreme Court anymore. Call me."

They parted in front of the building. Walking away, Macklin heard quick footsteps clicking on the sidewalk behind him. He whirled, closing his hand on the butt of the revolver under his coat.

"Go ahead. It'll save you fifty grand."

It was Donna. He let go of the gun. "Where's young Daniel Webster?"

"I sent him back to his office. Where can we talk?"

"I can't get to the money, and even if I could, you'd still have to prove there is any."

"It can be proved. But it isn't what I want to talk about."

They stood watching each other with the sidewalk traffic trickling around them. Under the sun her jowls were more evident and he could see the little cracks around her eyes under the thick mascara. But the eyes themselves were still pretty.

"My car," he said.

"Can't we go someplace for a drink?"

"No."

"Why not?"

"Because I don't and you can't."

"Since when do you care whether I drink or not?" she demanded.

"I never stopped."

"Don't try to tell me you still love me, you son of a bitch. If you do I'll take you for everything. I won't stop at half."

"I don't know that I ever did love you. But so many habits are fatal in my work you tend to hang on to the ones that aren't. I'll give you a lift home if that's where you're going."

"The long way."

She watched him check the Cougar over and let him open the door on the passenger side for her. He hadn't done that in ten years and she hadn't expected it in eight. They seemed to have fallen back into their premarital pattern in every respect but one. When they were moving up Woodward, she said, "I always liked this car. I want it."

"It's yours."

"Forget it. I'll take my part of the hundred."

"I want a less conspicuous car. I'll tell Klegg and he can work it out with your guy."

"Klegg doesn't look like a divorce lawyer."

"Goldstick looks like a lounge singer."

They passed through two traffic signals in silence. Lone dry leaves jiggled on the naked branches of trees planted in boxes on the sidewalks. The gutters were full of those already fallen.

"Mac, it's Roger."

"They bust him for drugs finally?" He had given up on their son months ago.

"No, he's off them. Working on it, anyway. He took your advice and went to that clinic you told him about. They locked him in. It was bad and they told me I saw the best of it."

"I didn't think he had it in him."

"He's only just stopped talking about killing himself."

"So what's the problem?"

"Now he wants to kill other people. For a living."

He was picking his way around a refrigerator truck double-parked on the right with its lights flashing. When they were back in their lane he glanced at her. She was looking straight ahead through the windshield.

"I wonder where he got the idea," she said.

"He tell you that?"

"I caught him playing with a gun in his room. He's been living at home since you moved out. He said he bought it off a man in a bar. When I told him he couldn't stay under my roof and keep a gun too he said that was fine with him, he'd soon have enough to buy a place of his own just as nice. Nicer. He said you did all right."

"He's just a kid."

"He's almost seventeen. How old were you?"

"Maybe he was just having fun."

"Not him. He's like you that way."

"He hates my guts."

"Obviously not, or he wouldn't be thinking of making your work the family profession. Maybe you can talk to him where I can't. You're his father."

"That doesn't cut anything with him. You give them a roof and three squares a day and put clothes on them and go into hock seeing them through school and it's not good enough anymore. Now you have to play baseball with them, go to father-and-son picnics. Be a pal. My dad never was, but I respected him."

"Yeah, and you turned out just swell." She dug a loose cigarette out of her purse and punched the dash lighter.

"He at home now?"

"He's staying at Lonnie Kimball's apartment on Lahser. They went to school together before Roger dropped out. You going to talk to him?"

"I've got too many other things to do right now. Maybe later."

"Later might be too late."

He said nothing. The lighter popped out and she lit up.

"Crack the window, okay? I like to see."

She lowered the glass on her side two inches. "If you talk to him today I'll tell Goldstick to forget the hundred grand."

"Roger isn't worth it."

"You're not his mother."

He swung left onto McNichols. "I'll see him tonight. I've got a full schedule all day."

"Things to do, people to kill."

Neither of them spoke the rest of the way to Southfield. Macklin dropped her off in front of their old home and took off with a squirt of rubber as soon as she slammed the passenger door. Minutes later he felt silly, but by then he was halfway back to Detroit.

Chapter Nine

NAME: Roy Blossom
AGE: 27 (approx.)
HEIGHT: 5' 10'' (approx.)
WEIGHT: 125–130
HAIR: Blond
EYES: Blue
SCARS: 1½'' bet. index and median fingers right hand, appendectomy, right side abdomen
CHARACTERISTICS: Head leans left, toes point out walking
FAMILY AND BIRTHPLACE: Tamaqua, Pennsylvania; father coal miner, mother's occupation unknown
OCCUPATION: Handyman, actor pornographic films, male model, mined coal while attending school
HOBBIES: _____

Seated at the tiny glass-topped secretary in his Harper Woods motel room, Macklin stared at the blank space on the neatly printed sheet before him, then wrote in: "Killing."

He flung down the pencil and read the information. Again he felt the sore lack of an efficient organization behind him. True, toward the end of his association with Boniface the background team had begun to get sloppy and the information nearly as sketchy as this, but at least they were professionals and the data they collected could be depended upon. He hated having to rely on the poor memory of a frightened woman who didn't even know where her tormentor—and Macklin's prey—was living.

Their second meeting had taken place on Belle Isle, where Macklin and Moira King had walked past the fountain and along the tourist paths while she twisted her hands on the strap of her purse and massaged her brain for useful details about Roy Blossom. She had explained that upon returning home from their first meeting she was seized with the certainty that someone had been inside her apartment in her absence. Nothing had been taken, but some small items were out of place and there was a smell about the rooms that told her they had been invaded. She had no doubt as to who it was and had immediately signed and mailed the two documents Macklin had given her. His subsequent call had been forwarded to a friend's house where she was staying. She was afraid to remain in her apartment.

"Has anyone been following you besides Blossom?" he had begun, without greeting.

"No, I—who else would be?"

"Did you tell anyone where we were going to meet yesterday?"

"No. Is something the matter?"

"Just that I haven't breathed safe air since I first heard your name. I hope you're telling me the truth. Being a woman doesn't buy you anything. It didn't with four others."

"Oh, Christ," she said. "I went to Uncle Howard to get Roy off my back and all I got was another Roy. Leave me alone, Mr. Macklin. Just leave me, period." She hung up.

He had called her back and soothed her and made the second appointment. Pegging the receiver, he had wondered if he would have bothered if the bulk of his hundred thousand dollars wasn't still hidden in his apartment where he couldn't get to it.

Now, fresh from the second meeting, he laid down the sheet containing the bare material on Blossom and picked up the photograph she had given him. It was two years old, scuffed and creased from many months spent rattling around forgotten in a drawer, but the details were sharp. It was an arrogant face, good-looking in a fussed-over way, with the lowered lids and the curled lip Macklin knew so well, having worn a similar expression in the early days of his career. He marveled that he had lived long enough to grow out of it. He committed the important features to memory, tore the picture and the hand-printed sheet into long strips, and set fire to them in the big glass ashtray the motel provided. The flame towered briefly, then abated, the strips darkening and curling. He broke up the ashes with the end of the pencil and dumped them into the midget wastebasket by his knee.

He counted six hundred dollars out of the thousand in his wallet and stashed three hundred in each breast pocket in case he lost the wallet, which he returned to his pants. The money was operating expenses provided by Moira King against the power of attorney. Then he put the room key in the ashtray for the maid to find.

From the drawer in the bedstand he scooped the Smith & Wesson in its holster and clipped it to his belt under his coat. Wearing it made him feel oddly vulnerable. He had never before carried a gun he had used once, had always been careful to ditch it, knowing he could lay hands on another without a history for the next assignment. Lugging around a weapon traceable to a dead Chinese in Westland was a one-way ticket to life in Jackson. But going unarmed was even more dangerous in his present situation, and he couldn't afford to go back to Treat for a replacement. Just going there the first time had been a risk. He had lost count of all the ironclad rules he had broken since visiting Klegg's office two days before.

Chapter Ten

Brown nudged his companion, who lurched forward to help the man with his suitcase. The man was one of the first out of the tunnel that led from the jet airliner into the concourse, thin and gray-faced in a tight black overcoat that reached below his knees and tinted glasses in the shadow of a gray felt hat with a broad brim. He looked as much like a killer as a killer could look. But before Brown's assistant could reach him, a fat woman with red-dyed hair wearing a fur coat swept past and threw her arms around the man's neck. He took off his hat to kiss her and they walked away toward the escalators, hugging each other's hips. Brown shrugged at his companion's dismay, uncorking a broad Slavic smile.

It was a big plane and they waited a long time while it emptied, stirring themselves for two more false alarms before the pilot came out followed by the copilot and three stewardesses. When an obvious plainclothes detective emerged handcuffed to a black woman, the two waiting men turned away.

"He must have missed his connection," Brown said.

"Inspires confidence." His assistant was a narrow American with deep sideburns and a weakness for orange neckties.

"After two failures I assume nothing."

"Mr. Brown?"

The pair turned. A man approaching sixty stood at their end of the tunnel, uncovering an impressive set of false teeth in an anxious grin. He had a big strapped leather suitcase on either side of him and his baggy overcoat gaped to expose a paunch gobleted in a green sweater. He wore black-rimmed glasses with round lenses and a maroon fur Tyrolean hat square on his head with a yellow feather in the band. His round face glistened pinkly.

"Mr. Brown?" he said again. He had a thick, furred accent.

Loath to ask the obvious question, Brown said, "Yes?"

The man gave a little pleased grunt and seized both suitcases and wobbled forward and set them down again, thrusting out a soft moist hand with bitten nails. "Dreadfully sorry to have kept you waiting, but I had my bags in the rear compartment and was forced to let everyone else pass down the aisle before I could go back for them." He wiggled the hand, as if the other hadn't noticed it. "I'm Mantis."

While the two shook hands a telephoto lens with a range 310 feet longer than any on the market blinked, freezing the pair amiably for the ages. The man behind it worked the shutter twice more, then melted back into the crowd around the metal detector and thumbed up a button on the lapel of his topcoat, murmuring into the grid pattern.

"Intertrap three, this is Intertrap two. Call Intertrap one and tell him contact has been made repeat contact has been made. Am continuing surveillance. Out."

The two men he had photographed were moving up the concourse, the third man struggling along behind with the newcomer's suitcases. The man with the camera waited until they passed, then hoisted the strap over one shoulder and fell into step several yards behind them, pulling a face at the silly kid things a grown man had to say and do in his business.

Sergeant Lovelady entered the office without knocking and found Inspector Pontier on the telephone again. The sergeant was retiring in fourteen months and most of his memories of his superior would be of him in his office with the receiver screwed to his ear. Lovelady spoiled every detective show his wife watched by carping about all these upper-level TV dicks who ran around trading lead with bad guys and never did any paperwork. He tipped the contents of his manila folder out onto Pontier's desk.

The inspector went on talking and fanned out the three black-and-white blowup photographs. He finished the conversation and hung up. "What's this?"

"Three possibles on those eyewitness descriptions at Klegg's building. Lyle Canaday, two arrests extortion, one conviction ADW. Philip Vernor, one suspended sentence aggravated assault. And Peter Macklin."

"Macklin, Macklin." Pontier stared at the third photo, a grainy shot taken with a long lens.

"FBI sent that one. Wait'll you see what's on the back."

The inspector turned it over and read the close typewriting on the heavy stock pasted to the back. After a minute he looked up.

Lovelady said, "You like?"

The big frame building on Lahser had been a farmhouse in the days, not so long ago, when everything north of Detroit was planted in corn and wheat. The farm had been subdivided and the big rooms partitioned off and converted into apartments. Macklin climbed a flight of open stairs wearily and knocked on 7.

His exhaustion was more mental than physical. He'd fought traffic all the way to Ypsilanti and back only to be told by an assistant director at the Center for Forensic Psychiatry that the patients' files were confidential and that even if Roy Blossom's address was recorded there it could not be given out. The killer had considered testing the Hippocratic Oath against Smith & Wesson, but it was too early in the search to start attracting that kind of attention. His head throbbed and his neck was sore.

He knocked again. A voice inside asked who was there.

"Roger?"

A pause, then floorboards shifted on the other side of the door. "Dad?"

Macklin confirmed the guess. The door opened.

"Roger?" he said again.

He hadn't been prepared for the change in his son's appearance. As tall as his father, the boy had always been more slender, but now he was emaciated, with deep hollows in his cheeks and his ribs showing where his striped tank top bagged at the armholes. His long black hair was dead, without luster, and his complexion was pale and mealy. He might have been a hundred years old. When he grinned at Macklin's confusion his face turned into a death mask.

"I don't feel half as good as I look."

Macklin, covering, said, "I heard you got off the stuff."

Roger stretched out his forearms for inspection. The wrists were peppered with healed-over scars but there were no fresh needle tracks.

"Can I come in?"

The boy walked away from the door. Macklin stepped inside and closed it behind him. The furniture in the single room was piled high with cast-off clothes and magazines. A portable Murphy bed stood in one corner and a stove and refrigerator crowded one end, both in need of scouring.

"Where's the bathroom?"

"Down the hall."

"That where your roommate is?"

"He's out." Roger dropped onto the sprung sofa. "I'm surprised you're in."

"I'm keeping quiet. My guts are still shaky."

Macklin watched his son light a cigarette, holding the match in two hands to avoid shaking out the flame. "I didn't know you were smoking."

"Keeps my mind off shit."

"Your mother told me you were here."

"She threw me out."

"That's not how she tells it."

"She send you?"

Wandering the room, Macklin had stopped before the only poster on the wall that he recognized, a reproduction of Hieronymus Bosch's painting of Hell. "You paying your share of the rent on this place?"

"Lonnie's carrying me. I'll pay him back later, when I get a place of my own."

"Proving yourself in this business takes time. You'll be lucky to take in a hundred bucks on your first job. A good gun will run you three times that."

"I got a good one that only cost fifty."

"Let's see it."

Roger flicked ash at the floor, got up, and took a foil-wrapped package out of the refrigerator.

"No good," Macklin said. "Moisture gets to the action."

"Not the way I wrapped it." Roger peeled back the foil and three layers of slick butcher paper. He hesitated before handing over the object inside.

"I'll give it back."

He laid the gun in his father's palm. It was a long-barreled Colt Woodsman .22 target pistol. Macklin ran back the action and broke out the magazine. It wasn't loaded. "Who sold you this piece of shit?"

"Twenty-two's a pro's gun," said Roger, snatching it back. He rammed home the empty clip.

"For a pro who knows what he's doing, and if he wants to be quiet about it," Macklin agreed. "I like 'em loud."

"Bring the cops down on your ass."

"Cops are the last thing you have to worry about on a job. The noise keeps the heroes away. A semiautomatic, Christ, you might as well leave bread crumbs. Leave shell casings behind, maybe get one caught in your cuff and they turn it out during the frisk."

"I don't wear cuffs."

"You even know the name of the guy you bought it from?"

"A guy in a bar. I see him there before. I know what business he's in."

"He sees this strung-out kid, figures he's found a good place to unload a piece with a past. Cops pull you over—way you look, I'd be tempted myself—pat you down, come up with a gun's been used in three robberies and a double homicide. Judge hangs life on you before you even taste blood."

Roger said nothing. He rewrapped the gun and put it back in the refrigerator.

Macklin said, "What you going to do about lining up work, take out an ad under 'Situations Wanted' in the *Free Press*?"

"I got a customer."

"Who? Somebody else you met in a bar?"

"Charles Maggiore."

This time Macklin was silent.

His son continued. "I went to his place. He was glad to see me, kept his accountants waiting while he talked to me out by the pool. Hey, I didn't know he was a hunchback. Stuff I read about him never said. Anyway, he said he'd call me when he had work for me."

"The son of a bitch."

"In a way I guess it was a compliment to you. Your genes, anyhow."

"He's using you to get back at me for helping spring Boniface. He got used to putting his feet up on the old man's desk."

Roger shrugged. "A start's a start."

Macklin unholstered his .38 and pointed it at his son. The young man was busy lighting a fresh cigarette from the butt of the last. His eyes widened, then narrowed. He finished and crushed out the butt under a threadbare track shoe. "Do it," he said. "It's the one thing will relieve these fucking cramps."

"I would, if a bullet from this gun weren't already in a dead man." He put it away. "You up for traveling?"

"Like where?"

"Just a short trip. Downtown Detroit."

Roger unsheathed the death's-head grin. "You taking me for a ride?"

"I might if I thought you were worth the gas. You got a telephone?"

"Downstairs."

"Get cleaned up or whatever you do when you're going out and meet me down there."

"I didn't say I was going."

But Macklin was already on the stairs.

Chapter Eleven

"**W**here we going?" Roger reached to put his cigarette out in the dashboard ashtray.

"Flick it outside."

He cranked down the window and released the glowing butt into the slipstream. They were passing a shopping center, red and blue neon washing the inside of the Cougar.

"You never answered my questions even when I was a kid."

"Yeah, I warped you by curbing your natural curiosity. Don't lay that Freudian crap on me."

"What's it like?"

"What's what like?"

"You know."

"Killing," Macklin said irritably. "If you're going to do it you've got to be able to say it. Or are you fixing to be one of these that call themselves liquidators?"

"I was just asking."

"After the first few times it's just work. That's why they pay you to do it. The ones that still get a jump out of it after five or six are ones to stay away from. Sooner or later they turn like Dobermans."

"I mean, is it like it is in movies?"

"Nothing ever is. Those movie killers' tongues are their best weapon."

"What's that mean?"

"They run on and on about what they're going to do to a

guy instead of just going ahead and doing it. What's the sense of telling someone what's going to happen to him if he's going to be dead in a minute? Real killers kill. They don't talk about it."

"You're talking about it."

"Could be I've been in it too long. When you get to thinking of yourself as something special, you're done. It happens sometimes."

"Well, what's it like the first time?"

"Wait until we get where we're going."

They circled the block of Lafayette and Brush twice before finding an empty meter and pulled in. Roger said, "There's a parking garage right over there."

"First things you give up in this work are parking garages and elevators and telephone booths. Let's go."

They mounted concrete steps and Macklin held the door for his son, who said, "I never been here before."

"Most people never have, breathing."

A young man wearing a white coat over a plaid shirt and necktie met them in the badly lit hallway. "Mr. Macklin? Lieutenant Cross said you called. I'm to give you the run of the place."

"Thanks."

The young man led the way around a corner and down an echoing flight of stairs. The air smelled of Lysol.

"Lieutenant?" Roger whispered.

"C.I.D.," said his father.

"How do you know a Detroit Police lieutenant?"

"Did you think we were all florists?"

At the bottom of the stairs their escort pointed the way and left them. As the pair walked, the odor of disinfectant gave ground slowly before a staleness that after a few steps had Roger shielding his nose with a hand. "Where are we?"

"Wayne County Morgue."

They passed through a room with chairs and a closed-circuit television screen into a larger room, where the stench burned Roger's newly revived olfactory nerves. Under bright fluorescent tubes five corpses lay naked on steel tables.

"Busy night," said Macklin.

"I get it." Roger looked around with a show of boldness. "I seen meat before."

The first table they stopped at supported a middle-aged black woman with pendulous breasts and a distended belly. Her face was oddly crumpled, like a collapsed balloon, the features almost concave.

"Suicide," Macklin said.

"How can you tell?"

His father took the dead woman's chin between thumb and forefinger and lifted it. They looked inside the loose flap of skin where her throat belonged. "Put a shotgun under her chin. When you blow out your brains and skull, your face falls in."

Now Roger noticed the woman's head had no top.

They visited the corpse of a little boy—"Drowned," announced the killer—hovered over a shapely young woman with multiple stab wounds in her breasts and abdomen, which Macklin pinched to show the edges of the cuts, and looked at a man in his late thirties with the back of his head caved in, the head lying flat as a paperweight on the table. Finally they stopped beside the body of a young Oriental whom at first Roger took to be a boy of eleven or twelve, but who, upon studying his face and the well-developed muscles under the smooth ivory skin, he realized was a man grown. He had two blue holes close together on his left breast and he was open from sternum to groin, exposing slabbed ribs and an empty cavity. A pile of red-and-purple entrails was heaped next to his hip. Macklin seized his son's wrist and shoved his hand into the pile.

Roger shouted and tried to pull loose. Macklin's grip was iron. The mess was slippery and cold as ice.

"Some you bring down with a deer rifle at six hundred yards," his father said. "Others you get right in close and smell the fear just before the knife goes in. Either way they wind up like this and that's what it's like."

The stench of the stirred guts rolled up into the boy's nostrils. Bile scaled his throat. Macklin's grim face was inches from his.

"They shit when you cut their throats, just dump right in their pants. You get used to the stink, though."

He held on for another moment before letting go. Roger jerked his hand out of the pile.

"You can catch a bus home on the corner." Macklin left.

Roger used the sheet folded at the foot of the table to mop off the dead blood and half-digested stomach contents. He sniffed his hand and threw up into a scrap bucket.

NAME: Peter Macklin

AGE: 39

HEIGHT: 5' 11½"

WEIGHT: 185

HAIR: Black, receding

EYES: Gray

SCARS: Recent powder burn, ½" above left eye; three bullet, ¼–1¼" diameter, left side thorax, upper right arm, behind right shoulder (exit); 6" knife, right side abdomen; 4" knife, 1" left of center and bisecting collarbone at 30° angle; bite, 2" diameter, left bicep; recent bullet mark, 2½", right hip.

CHARACTERISTICS: Slight forward tilt minimal arm movement walking, smiles rarely, no tics or mannerisms, ~~does not arm himself when not at work~~

FAMILY AND BIRTHPLACE: River Rouge, Michigan; father Eugene Macklin, truck dispatcher, strong-arm man Boniface family Detroit, Michigan; mother Georgia Murdock Macklin, housewife; no brothers or sisters

OCCUPATION: Killer

HOBBIES: None

ASSOCIATES: Donna Macklin, wife, 36, 10052 Beech Road, Southfield, Michigan; Roger Macklin, son, 16, address same;

~~Christine Lucarno, mistress, 6513 Oakwood Road, Dearborn,
Michigan, Apartment 12, file clerk, Ford Motor Company;
Umberto (Herb) Pinelli, friend, 4202 Greenfield Road, South-
field, Michigan, owner Clovis Haberdashers, 4200 Greenfield
Road, Southfield, merchant, retired killer~~

The old man returned the typewritten sheet to the manila folder.

Brown, anxious, said, "Satisfactory?"

"It is very spare. What, for instance, are these crossed-out items?"

"Corrections and updates. He no longer associates with the Lucarno woman, and this man Pinelli is dead, murdered in his shop after a struggle. That bit about going unarmed cost our last man his life. Our fault, I'm afraid. We try to stay abreast but the human factor is vexing."

"It is infuriating and exhilarating. It is my specialty. Ah." The maid came in and served their meal. Brown's assistant wrinkled his nose at the steaming patty on his plate. The man called Mantis inhaled, cheeks reddening with delight. "Meat loaf. A dish only Americans know how to prepare. You are a good host, Mr. Green."

"Brown. Mr. Green is my associate."

"Yes. Well, does it matter? We are three men with not a genuine name among us."

"I was told you favored meat loaf. Anya disapproved, but she's incapable of laying a poor meal. We can talk freely in front of her, incidentally. She has been with us since the Nine Hundred Days."

"Leningrad, yes. I helped relieve it. There was not a dog or a cat or a rat to be found in the city after the siege was lifted."

Brown raised his fork, only to lower it as the old man folded his hands and sank his collection of chins onto his chest with his eyes closed, moving his lips silently. The overhead light made blank circles of his eyeglasses. Green started and glanced at his superior, who shook his head.

Mantis stirred and became animated, unfolding his napkin and draping it over his swelling middle and eagerly cutting himself a morsel of meat loaf with the edge of his fork. "Superb! Just a bit heavy on seasoning, but it's better than any I've had since my last visit."

"It is better than any you have had," returned Anya in a heavy accent. The maid was tall and white-haired, with a nose that just missed being aristocratic and an old scar at the corner of her left eye. She finished serving and went back into the kitchen.

"America, it corrupts," the old man sighed.

Brown ate only vegetables, having forsworn meat in 1962, and studied his guest. Mantis had spread out the dozen shots of Macklin he'd found in the folder and gazed at them on the tablecloth as he chewed. His shoulders were rounded under the green sweater and he was bald to his crown, from which he grew his dull gray hair straight down and cut it off square at his collar. He drew out another typewritten sheet and read it, his eyes light and humorous behind the bifocals.

"Who is this woman Moira King?"

"Right now she's our only link to Macklin except Howard Klegg, and the police are watching him too closely," Brown said. "He moved out of his house in Southfield some weeks ago, and we haven't his current address. I doubt he's using it. Two separate attempts on his life have put him on his guard. He's a difficult man to kill at any time, but now he'll be doubly so."

"I am your last best hope."

"I wouldn't go so far as to say that."

"Of course you would not." The old man went on looking at him over the tops of his spectacles for a moment, then returned his attention to the sheet. "He has business with this Moira woman?"

"They are in contact."

"They are friends, lovers, what?"

"There is a connection. That's all you require."

Mantis slid everything back into the folder and held it out across the table. "I am not the man for you, Mr. White."

"Brown."

"You want one of these young lizard-eyed animals from Moscow, a robot in his twenties with his head full of Marx and Lenin that you can point like an arrow and know he will fly true and hit his target and obligingly destroy himself in the process. I would give you a list of names, but the list is always changing, as you can imagine. Instead I will thank you for the trip and for this excellent meat loaf—except for the rich seasoning—and go back home to Sofiya."

Brown didn't take the folder. "What do you want, Mr. Mantis?"

"Just Mantis, please." He laid the material between them on the table. "Information, Mr. Brown. Meat for the skeleton. When you have told everything I will decide how much I require and forget the rest. That I have attained this age in my profession is sufficient evidence of my powers of forgetfulness."

"Insubordination!" shrilled Green.

"I am not a subordinate." Mantis continued to watch Brown, who was staring thoughtfully at his plate.

"It's a clear violation of policy," he said then. "But I have latitude."

He spoke for ten minutes while the old man ate slowly and made no interruption.

When he was finished, Brown said, "How soon can you act?"

"A week perhaps." Mantis selected a warm roll from the basket on the table and tore it in half.

"That's too long. Macklin may have made his move by then."

"Not if he is the professional you have described. These matters require time. One does not . . ." He paused, made an exasperated face, and put down the roll half with which he had been sponging orange sauce from his plate. He bounced up and down on his chair, slapping an ample flank significantly while the others stared.

"Cowboy!" supplied Green finally.

"*Da*. One does not cowboy. It is this that has cost you two men. A man is not a target silhouette. If you are to penetrate his skin, you must wear it first. A week is the bare minimum. More if you want it to look like something other than murder."

"That's not important," said Brown.

"Excellent." Mantis popped the rest of the soaked roll into his mouth. "You know, the more I eat of this the better I find it. Does Miss Anya serve seconds?"

Chapter Twelve

Oral sex, he was sick of it.

Cranking the Moviola a little faster, the man seated behind the glass-topped desk shook his head at the tiny naked figures jerking and bobbing through the machine. He could never figure out how a copulating couple managed to kiss so ardently after just having had their mouths full of each other's genitals. He stopped cranking and drew over his memo pad and wrote: "Sam—Whatever happened to the good old missionary position? FYI, *The Joy of Sex*, diagram G-12."

He had never seen a copy of *The Joy of Sex* and didn't even know if that was how the diagrams were labeled. But the director would get the idea.

His intercom buzzed. He pressed the speaker button. "Yes, Angel."

His secretary's name was Pamela. He never let her forget that she had once appeared in films under the name Angel Climax. Coolly she replied: "There's a Mr. Macklin here to see you. Shall I send him in?"

He felt his blood drain into his feet.

"Mr. Payne?"

"Tell him I'm not in. I'm on vacation."

There was a pause. "He heard that, Mr. Payne."

He looked around the office for any exits he might have missed in four years in residence. In his late forties, Jeff Payne wore muttonchop whiskers and had his graying blond hair tinted and teased into curls to cover the thin spots. He jogged, stopped eating a dish as soon as it turned up on the cancer list, counted his cholesterol, and only went out with women under twenty-five. He hadn't celebrated a birthday in eleven years. He was contemplating his third-floor window when Macklin came in.

"Oh, hello, Mac." His eyes went automatically to his visitor's hands. They were empty. He felt himself starting to fall in on himself with relief.

"Jeff, I'm working for me now," said the killer. "Even if I weren't, I wouldn't come at you through your secretary."

"Hell, Mac, you didn't think I was afraid of that." He started to rise but couldn't find the bones for it and stretched out his hand sitting. Then he remembered the other's aversion to the gesture and let it drop. His palm left a wet mark on the desk's glossy surface. "Have a seat. How've you been?"

Macklin remained standing. "How's the dirty picture game?"

"In another year I can sue you for accusing me of being in it. Hard-core is out. There's no money in stag parties and old men in raincoats. This is the age of cable and videocassettes, software and soft porn. More story, fewer orgasms. Today's hip married couple wants something to get the juices flowing after the kids are in bed, but they want to think they're being enriched too. Hell, I burned five miles of mask-and-black-socks footage last month to make room in the warehouse for the new stuff. Nowhere to lay it off."

"Who's financing this big changeover?"

Payne, who had been warming to his own enthusiasm, felt the fear creep back in. "Is that why you're here? They always used to spot me at least a week before sending in the team."

"No. I told you my business isn't with you. I need a line on a model or an actor or whatever you're calling them now. He appeared in some films locally a couple of years ago."

"That's forever in this business." The other relaxed a little.

Not completely; he had been given his entire operation five years earlier for services rendered and rumor had it Macklin was responsible for the vacancy in management. "The burnout factor's pretty high when you have to get it up on demand."

"He's between films, been there for sixteen months. He may be just getting back into it."

"What's his name?"

"Roy Blossom."

"Know his screen name?"

"What's that mean?"

"Johnny Wadd. Will Hung. Peter Prong. Back then they didn't exactly want their baptismal handles up in lights. I used to go with an actress called herself Joy Trail."

"I didn't think to ask. Last time I saw one of the things the actors weren't using any names at all."

"Those were good days. There wasn't any art to the things but they had a raw vitality you don't see today."

"Jeff, I could stand here all day reminiscing about the golden age of skin flicks."

Payne got the hint. He pressed the intercom button and asked Pamela to look up Roy Blossom in the talent file.

"I got a short here's got to be shot all over again," said Payne while they were waiting, slapping the Moviola. "They're always going down on each other, plenty of wet close-ups. I'd have to unload it on a Woodward Avenue grindhouse to get anything back on my investment. Care to see?"

"No."

They waited some more. When the intercom buzzed Payne jumped on it.

"No Blossom," reported the secretary. "I've got a Bliss and three Blooms."

"Thanks, Pam. Sorry, Mac."

"Where else would he apply?"

"I can give you some names. But we're the biggest in

town. If he's making the push to get back in, we'd have his résumé on file."

"Okay. Thanks, Jeff. You didn't see me."

"See who?"

After Macklin went out Payne gave the Moviola crank a few more turns, then pushed away the machine and sat back, feeling wrung out. He made a mental note to borrow some money to pay off his debts.

Macklin used a telephone inside a service station to dial Howard Klegg.

"I expected you to call before this," said the lawyer.

"I've been busy. Anything yet on who signed the paper on me?"

"No. I told you, Boniface came up empty. How's it going with Moira?"

"I'm not into talking about my work with anyone who happens to ask."

"Okay, okay. I've got a meeting in my office with your wife and her lawyer tentatively set for three this afternoon. Can you make it?"

"Yeah, I guess so."

Klegg paused. "Can you come early, say two?"

"How come?"

"Not over the phone."

Macklin watched the fat woman cashier make change for a customer. "What's it going to be this time, a bomb? Or is that too run-of-the-mill?"

"For Christ's sake, Macklin!"

"Two o'clock." He broke the connection.

He was there at one. The stairwell still smelled of burning trash and the fireproof paneling was scorched and bowed slightly outward. He climbed the three flights with his gun in his hand, making sure the hallway was deserted before he put away the weapon and swung the door wide.

Klegg was out to lunch. His secretary, a trim woman of forty with tawny hair caught with combs behind her ears and a white ruffled blouse under a tailored tan jacket, told Macklin he could go into his office and wait. Her face betrayed no memory of the commotion surrounding the killer's last visit. He let himself into the sanctum.

"Mr. Macklin."

He tore the .38 out from under his sport coat. A black man with a graying fringe was sitting behind the lawyer's desk with his hands flat on top. He had gray eyes and wore a suit that fit him well.

"Put it up."

This was a different voice. Macklin shifted his attention slightly left, to a revolver of the same make and caliber in a fat hand belonging to a broad man wearing a yellow sport coat in need of a press. His face was flat and pockmarked and he wore his red hair in a bowl cut.

Macklin said, "Uh-uh."

The man behind the desk lifted one of his hands, palming a leather badge folder. "I'm Inspector Pontier. That's Sergeant Lovelady, my partner. When Klegg made the appointment for two I said to the sergeant you'd be here at one. We've been waiting since noon. This is why your city income tax is so high. I don't guess you have a permit for that gun."

Macklin said nothing. He and Lovelady watched each other. The sergeant's eyes might have been two more pits with paint on them.

The black man gestured with the folder before putting it away. His partner hesitated, then elevated his barrel. Macklin kept his level.

"You First," Pontier said. "It's a game most of us quit playing after we get our first hard-on. The cops and robbers business is just grown-up kid stuff. It's okay, Sergeant. Mr. Macklin is a professional. He doesn't shoot police officers."

After a space the sergeant returned his weapon to a clip

under his left arm. Macklin hung on another moment before he started to feel silly, like the only person with his clothes on in a nudist camp, and leathered his own. Pontier spoke again.

"Don't blame Klegg. He knows an accessory rap would be just the hole we'd need to get in with both hands and start digging. It isn't easy being a crook at his level. You can't just run when things fall in and you never know when things are going to start falling. Sit down."

"Thanks, I sat in the car on the way here."

Pontier made a shrug. "They used to say the criminal always returns to the scene of the crime. It's still true a lot of the time. Problem is you can't always spot him. But the minute I saw that burned body at the bottom of the stairs the other day I said to myself, this one's coming back. Lawyers don't get much off-the-street trade and justice isn't dispensed in one day. Also people don't change lawyers unless they do something really stupid like grabbing the judge's necktie in court. It's human nature. So I knew you'd be back."

"That your evidence?"

"Well, there's a little more to it, like a clear match between eyewitness descriptions and the picture and stats in your FBI file. Hell of a time prying that away from the Feds. They don't like to admit they employ killers from time to time. You did an impressive job aboard the Boblo boat last August."

"I was out of town last August."

"On Lake Erie, to be precise. Anyway, that one's closed. Nobody alive to file a complaint. All I'm interested in is what you did to Keith DeLong to make him so mad at you."

"I never heard of him."

"His name was in the *Free Press* this morning."

"I'm self-employed. I don't get much time to read."

"Self-employed at what? Free-lance camera repair? We checked with Addison Camera. You quit first of September."

"I'm a human relations consultant. I solve people's personal problems for a fee."

Pontier and Lovelady laughed together. The sergeant's bray fairly shook the new window in its frame.

"What wasn't in the Freep this morning," went on the inspector, suddenly deadpan, "is that after his discharge from the Marines and while he was laid off from his construction job, DeLong filed an application for employment with a mercenary recruitment office the FBI has been trying to shut down for eighteen months. Things have been calm for a while and his application wasn't processed. What we have is a man trained by the government to kill, who is looking for similar work on his own and not having a hell of a lot of luck. Now, what fraternal organization with a five-letter name beginning with *M* might find his talents worthy of exploiting?"

"Get to the point, Inspector."

"The point is you don't quit places like Addison Camera that are affiliated with this organization I'm talking about. If you try they get awful mad."

Macklin leaned his hands on the desk.

"I'm not saying I was anywhere near here when DeLong fried himself," he said. "But if I were, am I under arrest for watching him do it?"

"I'm not saying you were anywhere else," said Pontier. "But if you weren't, you wouldn't be a material witness to an attempted homicide."

"You don't have enough to take me into custody."

"I could take you down just for carrying that peashooter."

"You could try."

Lovelady made a noise.

Pontier said, "You life-takers make my ass ache. You think you're the only ones cross that line. How many is it now, Sergeant?"

"Six."

"When I met him it was four," he told Macklin. "He'd've

made lieutenant long before this if he didn't have so many notches on his department piece. When I took over the squad I asked for the personnel file on every plainclothes-man on the force. When I finished reading Lovelady's I put in for him first. I.A.D. stuck him under hack for three bad shoots, but he managed to squeak through with restricted duty and two suspensions without pay. I wanted at least one man on the detail who could work a trigger without stopping to wonder what would happen to him afterwards. So don't go huffing and puffing around him. He's got a shield and you don't and that's the only difference between you."

Macklin took the sergeant's measure. Lovelady's face gave up as much expression as the plate of cottage cheese it resembled.

Pontier got to his feet. "We'll leave it there for now," he said. "I promised Klegg we'd be gone before he got back from lunch. Oh, you wouldn't know anything about a young Chinese man who was found dead in Westland day before yesterday."

"I don't know any *live* Chinese."

"Okay. It's just that he was shot twice with a .38, and the Westland Police are having the same trouble identifying him that we had with DeLong."

"I'm not the only one in Detroit carries a .38."

"No. But you use it more than most. I was just asking. We'll talk again." He moved toward the door. Lovelady stepped over to open it.

Macklin said, "Aren't you going to warn me not to leave town?"

Pontier chuckled.

Out in the hall, Lovelady said: "It didn't work. He ain't some kid we jerked down for stealing tape decks from cars."

"With those guys you can't ever tell." Pontier rang for the elevator.

"I don't look the part. You can take one look at me and know I never fired my piece off the police range."

"You're closer to it than the killer cop I modeled you after."

"I thought you made him up."

"No, he's real."

The elevator doors opened and they stepped aboard. "How come he ain't on the detail?"

"Killing's easy. It's the not killing takes brains and guts." They descended.

Chapter Thirteen

"I think we've made real progress," Klegg announced, rising from behind his desk and shaking hands with Goldstick. "That nonsense about the hundred thousand dollars was the only real stumbling block."

Goldstick smiled. "Judge Flutter will turn cartwheels when he hears."

"I'd give up my license to practice law to see that."

"Coming, Donna?" Goldstick asked.

"I'll catch up with you." She was standing close to Macklin. They glanced at Klegg, who busied himself with things on his desk. Macklin touched her elbow and they moved to the far end of the office.

"Roger told me you talked to him yesterday," she said.

"You're right. He does hate your guts."

"Well, he hates guts. Think it worked?"

"I don't know. It's so hard to tell with him. He really is like you. Thanks, Mac. For trying."

"The price was right."

Her eyes were still young in the fleshy face. She took them from his and opened her purse.

"I found these yesterday when I was cleaning. I thought maybe you'd like to have them." She handed him a small bundle of yellowed and curling envelopes bound with a rubber band. "There isn't much. You were never one for getting and writing letters."

"You were cleaning?"

She smiled then, a little stiffly. "I'm getting neat as all hell. You wouldn't know the place. I've enrolled in a health club too. Going to see if I can take off a few pounds." She paused. "I'm job hunting. First time in my life."

"How's the hunting?"

"Aside from the fact I'm too old and don't have any skills, it's just peachy. The interviewers are all very courteous and polite. You never lied to me with that kind of grace."

"I only lied to you about my work. Nothing else."

"What about Christine?"

He looked at her. She met his gaze, then looked away.

"I found a note from her you forgot to tear up. One of these things you leave on someone's pillow. Pretty hot stuff, Mac. Is that what you liked? You never told me."

"What's it matter, Donna?"

"Nothing. Now. I just never thought I was that dense."

"You were that drunk."

"I took my first drink the day I found out what you did for a living."

"You did it to celebrate finding a reason. You'd been looking for one for years."

Silence crackled. He remembered the bundle of letters and slipped off the rubber band. One of the older envelopes contained a fold of green construction paper pasted over with pictures of flowers cut out of a seed catalogue. Inside was a legend scrawled in purple crayon.

" 'Roses are red,' " he read.

"Roger made it for you that time you were in the hospital," she said. "He was four."

"I'd forgotten it." He looked at it a moment longer, then returned it to its tattered envelope and shuffled through the rest of the stuff. He replaced the rubber band and handed back the bundle. "Keep it for me, will you? Throw it out if it gets in your way. I do a lot of moving around and it would just get lost."

She put it back in her purse.

"I guess I should ask how you are," she said. "But I don't care."

"Thanks for thinking of me with the letters."

"Where can I reach you? I mean, if Roger . . . "

"Call Klegg."

When she left, the lawyer stopped straightening his desk and looked down the length of the office at Macklin. "You talked to Pontier?"

"I did. If you weren't my lawyer I'd kill you."

"That's been said to a lot of lawyers. It's why you never pick up a paper and read about one being found in a car trunk at Metro Airport with a hole in his head. He got on to you somehow. I knew he didn't have any proof, he was acting too cagey. I didn't think it would do any harm if you talked."

"You could have told me. I came in here wearing a gun I could have gone down a long time just for having."

"Would you have come if I did?"

"No."

Klegg spread his hands. "I'm in a vulnerable business. I have to put up a show of cooperation. As careful as I am there is always something a good investigator could get hold of if he digs. Up to now I haven't given any of them a reason to want to. When I do it won't be because some hoodlum I never heard of set himself on fire in my building."

"Pontier explained that."

"Question is did you believe it."

"Next time tell me," Macklin said.

The thin old man lowered himself into his chair. When he did that he seemed to grow broader and more substantial. "How's Moira?"

"I said I don't talk shop."

"I heard you. I just want to know how she is."

"She's in trouble deep."

"If I didn't know that I wouldn't have had her find out the two of you exist in the same world."

"I'm just for dusting off when you need me," Macklin said. "Then it's back up on the dark shelf."

Klegg wasn't listening. He cut a thin smile at one of the chairs arranged before the desk. "She used to come in and sit there while her father was interviewing a client he didn't want her to meet. Her feet barely reached the floor. I spent almost as much time with her in those days as Lou did. His wife hemorrhaged after birth and he raised her alone. If she'd had a mother she might not have had the problems she did. But she's making her way back now." He looked at Macklin. "I want this man Blossom out of her life."

"You mean, you want him out of his own."

"Remember I never said that."

"Lawyers," said Macklin, on his way out.

In his hotel room the old man double-locked the door and inspected the room and bath for unwanted visitors. There were none. He had already checked out the view from his window and satisfied himself that there were no fire escapes or nearby roofs from which an intruder might gain entrance. He shrugged off his overcoat and hung it with his hat on a hook in the closet, then opened one of his big suitcases on the bed. From it he took a small bottle of red-and-black capsules. In the bathroom he swallowed one and chased it down with water.

Next he drew the curtains over the window, dumped the contents of the manila folder out onto the bed, and used Scotch tape to fix the dozen five-by-seven glossy photos to the mirror over the bureau in two neat horizontal rows. Most of them had been shot with a long lens, but there was one formal mug and a family portrait several years old, the latter cadged from the files of a studio photographer who owed someone a favor. The old man sat on the foot of the bed drinking the rest of his water and gazing at the pictures. Two showed the man getting into and out of his car, a silver Cougar. One included a clear view of the license plate.

Someone rapped at the door. He got up and used the peephole, lowered his bifocals to focus through it. He recognized the bellboy who had brought up his suitcases and unlocked and opened the door.

"Sir, you said to bring this up the minute it came." The young man held out a package the size of a shirt box wrapped in brown paper and bound with string.

"Thank you." The old man accepted the package and closed the door on the bellboy, who was staring down at the seventy-five cents in his hand.

The old man relocked the door and sat down at the secretary to tear off the wrapping. He opened the pasteboard box and separated the Styrofoam inside from a slim pistol built on a magnesium frame with a bare grip. It was a 7.65-millimeter Walther of a special design, weighing less than eight ounces. After inspecting the action he laid it aside and turned to the rest of the items in the package.

He used a penknife to pry the top off the first of the jacketed cartridges. The brass nose was hollow, lined with lead. He opened the heavy little plastic bottle he had brought and used a glass eyedropper to insert a bright wobbly silver globule of mercury in the bullet cavity. Last he lit a squat candle he had bought downtown and dropped wax into the cavity to seal it. He reassembled the cartridge, tamping down the bullet with gentle taps of a small yellow nylon-headed mallet, put down the cartridge, and selected another from the box. He spent the next half hour filling a full pistol load with mercury.

It was simple physics. Upon impact inertia forced the mercury forward, splintering the lead and the brass jacket and opening a hole in unprotected flesh large enough to let daylight through. Thus a hit anywhere in the body guaranteed a fatality from massive blood loss, if indeed it did not kill instantly. It was safer to fire than the old dum-dum, which had been known to separate in the gun's barrel and cause a backfire, and it required less charge than a magnum load, heightening accuracy.

Finishing, Mantis wiped his glasses. He disliked the mercury load for aesthetic reasons and had no plans to use it. But only a cowboy declined to back himself up.

Chapter Fourteen

A door swung open, coming up against the wall with a crash that knocked a picture loose from the wall on the other side. In the same instant a young woman hurtled through the opening and sprawled across the bed just inside when her knees touched the edge. Behind her, almost as explosively, entered a young blond man dressed in a heavy turtleneck and jeans, who hauled her off the bed by one wrist and spun her into his body and touched the razor point of a knife with a long, slim blade to the underside of her chin.

"Take off your clothes," he commanded.

The room was washed in alternating red and blue light from a neon sign outside the window. As the woman obeyed, fumbling with the buttons and zippers, the skin she bared added a golden underlay to the liquid hues. When she was naked, her nipples and pubic hair were very dark in the shifting light.

The sex was slow but brutal and punctuated by gasps and grunts, the lovers' wet bare flesh reflecting the neon colors. When it ended in a cataclysmic double orgasm, the screen went empty. A loose end of film fluttered in the projector.

"Run it again," Macklin said.

The projectionist rewound the film. The killer sat alone in a dark theater that smelled of dust and old sweat, as if the odor had leaked off the thousands of miles of scenes of sexual intercourse that had panted and slobbered across the flyblown screen. Even his seat felt sticky.

The film started again with a brief title and credits. Roy Blossom's name didn't appear, but from his first entrance there was no mistaking those sneering good looks. As before, Macklin ignored the other players and concentrated on Blossom's movements. Very early in his career the killer had learned the relative unimportance of facial features in the stalking of a mark; since the hunter spent most of his time behind his game, it was a man's distinctive carriage, the way he held his head and swung his arms, his gait and mannerisms that counted. Once you had them down and if you didn't let your mind wander, losing your man in a crowd was next to impossible. He observed his quarry in silence and took no notes. Pieces of paper with things written on them were always getting lost and being found by the wrong people. He had spent many long hours developing a photographic memory, and it was so much a part of him now he no longer had to work at remembering a thing of importance.

Blossom had good moves and an athletic build, a runner's body, cylindrical and gently muscled. What it would lack in strength it would make up for in endurance. He was younger than Macklin, but Macklin was used to youthful opponents. Sheer longevity had dictated that as a necessity. He noted with some small jealous satisfaction that although Blossom was an energetic lover, his penis was small by comparison to his fellow male performers.

When the motel room door onscreen crashed open a second time, he decided he'd seen enough. He stood, throwing a hard black shadow across the scene, and called his thanks to the projectionist in his alcove above the balcony.

"Tell Jeff Payne we're even," he added.

He blinked in the afternoon sunlight outside the theater, breathing in fresh air and auto exhaust from Woodward Avenue. He hadn't asked Payne where he had found one of Blossom's films from two years ago, had accepted his invitation to view it without question. He took results on face value.

Now Macklin knew everything about his man he had to, except where to find him.

The car was still there.

Moira King had first spotted it in her rearview mirror on her way home from her cubicle at Michigan Bell and had noticed it again a couple of turns later, and now here it was, still parked across the street from her apartment building in Redford Township. She had no knowledge of makes or models but it was a distinctive vehicle in color and style and she knew she wasn't mistaken. Someone was sitting behind the wheel, but the angle of the roof cut off her view of his head. She saw only a jacketed arm resting on the window ledge.

Turning away from her apartment window, she clenched a fist and willed herself to calmness. She wished she had Macklin's telephone number. All he had given her was a post office box. The way the mails were it could be the next day before a note reached it, and even then there was no telling how much time would pass before he read the note. She wished he'd call. She hadn't heard from him since their meeting at the zoo and all her suspicions about his genuineness were rushing back.

Maybe he and Howard Klegg were in it together. She had been stupid to think she could come to Uncle Howard for help after all those years with no contact. He had been kind to her when she was small, but people with no hearts at all were soft on puppies and children, and she had outgrown her innocence with a vengeance. She wondered if she were being made to pay for not attending her father's funeral. His death had come at a time when she had grown to hate everything he represented, and by then she was so deep in the underground film business that there had seemed no coming back.

She mixed whiskey and ginger ale in a tall glass in the kitchenette and carried it into the living room that made up the apartment with bath, pausing to look out the window once again. The car was still there, the arm too. She sat on the sofa and kicked off her shoes to tuck her feet up under her. It seemed important to behave as if it were just another early evening at home. She didn't know why.

For the first time in a long time she wanted a man. Completely, sexually. It surprised her. She had never had time for the rhetoric or martial emotions of the so-called women's movement, but she had endorsed the notion that a woman could survive without male protection and companionship. After Roy and that endless parade of faceless men with organs that stood up on command in the studios around town, she had developed a contempt for the whole sex. She had known other actresses who shared that contempt and who had tried to convert her to lesbianism, but the sexual act itself had become repugnant to her, caught up with memories of hot airless rooms and filthy beds whose sheets were changed not nearly so often as the reels in the cameras, and of the physical pain of too much love made to loins too dry. Those women were just an extension of the men they despised. She had taken comfort from her newfound celibacy. That she could feel the desire again she considered a betrayal on the part of her hormones.

So she no longer had the superiority of her contempt, and now that her home had proven less than impregnable she had lost even that small security. She hadn't felt so vulnerable since her first audition, when she had taken off her clothes for an excitable Arab armed with a cheap Polaroid camera. She dreaded nightfall.

Her glass was empty. She didn't remember drinking its contents. On her way back to the kitchen for a refill she pulled aside the curtain again. The car was there. The arm was gone.

She looked up and down the street. It was deserted but for

more parked cars and a pair of half-grown boys walking along the far sidewalk in football uniforms, cleats dangling from around their necks. She peered again at the car. She could see down to the cushion on the driver's seat and it was empty. The glass in her hand creaked from the tension of her grip.

The door buzzer rasped.

She dropped the glass. It bounced once on the padded carpet and rolled under the telephone stand. For a blind moment her eyes searched the apartment for other ways out and lighted on the window. But it was a two-story drop and she was weak from not eating, her appetite spoiled by constant fear. The fall would kill her.

The buzzer sounded again. It had the odd effect of rearranging her senses. She clawed at the stubborn drawer in the telephone stand, breaking a nail before it came out with a squawk. She took out the .25 semiautomatic pistol.

She had purchased it in a Grand Avenue pawnshop after the apartment had been broken into. The black man behind the counter had barely glanced at the false signature on the State of Michigan paperwork, then showed her how to load and operate the small square gun.

She jacked a cartridge into the chamber the way he had demonstrated and approached the door. She was conscious of her ankles shaking, but the hand holding the weapon was strangely steady.

The buzzer was going off a third time when she released the lock and stepped back, calling for her visitor to enter. She almost shrieked the welcome. The door opened. She squeezed the trigger at waist level.

Then the door was open wide and a body was charging through it and a hand closed on hers and wrenched the gun from her grasp, nearly taking her finger with it before the trigger guard pulled free. She screamed and kicked and a heavy backhand came swooping around in deceptive slow motion and a light exploded in the side of her head. Her knees lost their tension and she fell hard on her back on the floor.

The details of the room and of her attacker turned viscous then. She blinked her eyes to clear them, and as the edges sharpened she lay looking up the incredible length of a man in a checked sport coat, at tired features near the ceiling and a sharp widow's peak. He examined the small pistol disgustedly before flinging it onto the sofa.

"Next time remember to take off the safety."

"Mr. Macklin." She lay unmoving. "I thought—"

"Yeah. No wonder he had no trouble following you. I could've done it on foot."

"That silver car is yours?"

"I got tired of looking for him. If you're right about him, he'll come here sooner or later."

Still, she made no move to rise. He got the hint then, and with an expression of exasperation he bent over her and extended a hand. She took it and he pulled her up, supporting her back with the other. When she was on her feet, she fell against him and held on for a moment before they separated. He was harder than he looked, with little of the middle-aged softness she had expected.

His exhausted-looking eyes prowled the room. "Find anything missing yet?"

"No." Self-consciously she adjusted her sweater and skirt and straightened her hair. "I don't have many valuables and they're all here."

"I meant, like clothes. Underwear."

"Good God, no. Roy was always normal about that kind of thing. He's a maniac, not a pervert."

"You never know how a man will think after the shrinks get through rooting inside his skull. You want to tell me the rest of it?"

"What rest?"

He looked around some more. "You sleep here?"

"Yes. The sofa unfolds into a bed. What rest of it?"

He jerked his chin at the sofa. She stared at him. He pulled his lips out with a disgusted smack. "Sit."

She sat. She was conscious of her stockinged feet and put her shoes back on. He remained standing.

"There's a paper out on me," he said. "I've had them out on me before but that's when I was connected and it usually wasn't hard to figure out who issued them. Since I first heard your name there have been two tries, and nobody I've talked to knows who set them up. That isn't normal. I don't know what you've read or heard about *omertà*, but that oath of silence always was a crock. Six hours after a hit order comes down every little rat on the street knows most of the particulars. But this one's been a blank wall from the word go. Secrets get kept only two ways. The one I'm fondest of is only one person knows it, in this case the guy who's hiring the shooters. Or the woman who's doing it."

"Are you accusing me?"

"Hell, lady, you just tried."

"I thought you were Roy! Why would I want to kill you?"

"Why isn't important. People die all the time without knowing why."

"What's the other way secrets get kept?"

"By letting the man you're keeping them from ask all his questions of the wrong people. I don't like that at all. Too complicated."

"You don't think it's me," she said.

"What makes it I don't?"

"Because you're letting me sit on this sofa next to the gun I tried to use on you just now."

He made a little movement and she was looking at a heavy revolver in his right hand. He put it away.

She broke apart then. Bitter sobs climbed her throat, choking her.

"I should've just left town," she croaked. "I shouldn't have gone to Uncle Howard."

He said, "I'm rustproof. Waterworks fall short with me."

"Get out."

He didn't move.

She was on her feet then, coming at him with her nails out. "Get out! Get out of my apartment! Now!"

He caught her wrists and held on, his jaw muscles standing out from the strain of keeping her nails from his eyes. She collapsed against him then, sobbing uncontrollably. His arms went around her.

"*My* apartment," he reminded her. "You signed it over to me along with everything else, remember?"

Her sobs broke into a short feeble hiccup of a laugh. He held on, her wet face buried in his chest.

Chapter Fifteen

The old man loaded the pistol, returned it to its box, and rewrapped the package loosely, looping the string around it. Then he unpacked his clothes from one of the suitcases into the bureau drawers and put the package in the suitcase. He spun the combination lock, secured the straps, and hoisted the case onto the top shelf in the closet.

He napped, setting his folding travel alarm for an hour. He hadn't trusted hotel wake-up services since a dilatory clerk had almost made him late for his first murder. He took off his shoes and glasses and fell asleep quickly atop the bedspread and awoke at the alarm's preliminary click. By then it was dark out. He washed his face in the bathroom, came out, sat down at the secretary, and read the typewritten information once again from start to finish. Then he peeled the pictures off the bureau mirror and placed them in the manila folder with the report. He tore it in half, then quarters, then eighths, and continued tearing the pieces until the desk was littered with confetti. Finally he swept them into the ice bucket provided by the hotel and took it into the bathroom and flushed the pieces down the toilet a handful at a time.

When the last of the scraps had disappeared, he rinsed out the bucket, swallowed another red-and-black capsule, put on his hat and coat, and went out. In the elevator he removed his hat for a middle-aged woman in a green pantsuit, who glanced at him once, then returned her attention to the numbers flashing over the doors.

• • •

"L.A. Police, Inspector."

Pontier glanced up at Sergeant Lovelady, found nothing in the ravaged slab of a face, and accepted the big envelope, pushing aside the duty roster to make room on his desk for the contents. He looked at the front-and-profile mug of the man he knew as Detroit John Doe No. 106, read: "Robert Lai, a/k/a Robert Lye, Bob Lee, Lee Shang, Shang Lee, Chih Ming Shang, Shadow Dragon." The physical description was a clear match with the corpse in the morgue. Pontier turned to the rap sheet and goggled at the dense block of Teletyped information. Lovelady capsulized.

"Fourteen arrests assault, ADW, assault with intent, attempted homicide, suspicion of homicide, extortion. One conviction ADW, he pulled half a year in Q. The deadly weapon was his hands. He was a registered black belt or whatever they call it in kung fu."

"Mobbed up?"

"The Chinese gangs in L.A. and Frisco. This is as far east as he's worked, if the dope is straight."

"What the hell was he doing here?"

"All the label on his skivvies told the Westland cops is he shopped in Los Angeles."

"How do they feel about us mixing in?"

"Stiff's a nonlocal, there's no heat to clean it up. It's all ours with the original wrapping. I'm waiting on a call from the Feds."

"What's the holdup?"

Lovelady made an expression that for him was a grin. "Computer's down. They said."

"Fucking machines. Think they've got a hold on this Dragon character's file?"

"All I know is I spent most of my call on hold. They play music now. I bet I heard 'You Are the Sunshine of My Life' sixteen times before they came back on to tell me about the computer."

"Jesus. I'm putting you in for a commendation."

"More like disability."

Pontier reached for the telephone. "What's the regional director's name?"

"Burlingame. Randall Burlingame."

Light from the street lamp outside the window fell short of the ceiling, leaving a black hollow above the filmy gray oval. On other nights Moira would lay there imagining she was at the bottom of a deep shaft and that the light was leaking in through an escape tunnel at the side. It was a comforting fantasy while it lasted, but then the sun would rise and the ceiling would show, and she would have to face the fact that there were no escape tunnels.

But tonight she lay with her head in the hollow of a man's naked shoulder and one leg crooked over a hard hairy stomach with a stubborn pad of fat around the base, and the space around her under the covers was very warm, almost hot. She could hear the dull measured thud of his heart and feel his breath stir her hair. His breathing was slightly uneven and she could tell he was awake. She bent her leg further, pressed closer. She felt him gasp.

"Did I hurt you?"

"I bruised some ribs on that side a couple of months ago." His voice was a deep rumble.

"I'm sorry. It didn't show earlier."

He disengaged himself and peeled back the covers. She clutched his arm. "Do you have to leave?"

"I'm not much for talking after. Sorry." He reached for his clothes on the chair next to the bed.

"I wasn't thinking of talking."

"I'm not much for more than once a night, either. I need sleep more than most people."

"Why not sleep here?"

"I'm not doing any good here. In bed with you I'm an unloaded gun. I've got to be able to move around."

"Do you think Roy's close?"

"You do. That's why you hired me." He tucked in his shirt and clipped the Smith & Wesson to his belt, snugging the butt into the small of his back. Then he put on his sport coat.

"It's cold out tonight," she said. "Don't you have an overcoat?"

"If I get too comfortable I'll fall asleep. I'll be in the car. I don't think he can get inside the building without me seeing, but if anything happens, throw something through that window."

He started for the door. She got out of bed naked and threw her arms around his chest. The revolver prodded her belly. "Thank you."

"It wasn't that great." He stood unmoving.

"It was on time."

"Don't make anything more of it than it is," he said. "I don't want to find any cards with cute animals on them in my post office box."

She said, "You're trying too hard to be cold."

"Not hard enough or I'd be in the car by now."

She let go.

"Lock the door behind me." He went through it.

She twisted the lock and slid the chain into its socket. She heard his footsteps going away then. The air was cold on her bare skin. She padded back to bed and drew the covers over herself, snuggling into the warm hollow he had left in the sheet. She lay at the bottom of a deep shaft with light coming in through the side tunnel.

A small housing tract faced Moira King's apartment house across the street. The lawns were freshly sodded and the buildings smelled of sawdust and fresh concrete. Only half of them were occupied, the rest still posted. In the doorway of one of the unsold units the young man stood shifting his weight from one foot to the other and warming his hands in the side pockets of his navy peacoat. His cruel good looks were hidden by shadow and by his raised collar and the blue knit cap he had drawn over his ears and down to his eyebrows. He liked the outfit, which he had appropriated from wardrobe on one of his films. He had been told he looked like a Scandinavian sailor in it.

When the man in the checked sport coat came out of the lighted lobby across the street he pressed farther back into shadow, but after a quick glance around the man crossed at an angle away from where he was standing and got into a long low car parked at the curb. The young man waited. When after five minutes the car showed no sign of starting up and driving away, he eased out of the doorway. In the light of the corner street lamp he saw the man's head resting on the back of the driver's seat.

He looked up to where the light reflected dully off the window of Moira's apartment. He thought he saw the curtain move and remained still in the darkness on the unfinished lawn. For ten minutes he stayed unmoving. But the curtain didn't stir again and with a final glance in the direction of the parked car he turned and headed down the block and around the corner to where his own car was standing. In his right coat pocket the handle of the closed knife felt cool to the touch.

The old man half lay in the backseat of his rented Oldsmobile, following the young man with only his eyes as he passed, trailing vapor in the crisp air. When the pedestrian was out of sight he returned his gaze to the Cougar parked a full block up the street. He had already confirmed the license number through the infrared glasses on the seat beside him.

He had found the Cougar empty when he took up his vigil and had been there when the young man had appeared and taken his position in the doorway of the empty house. Again using the binoculars, he had matched the newcomer's gait and features to the description Mr. Brown had provided. When Macklin had emerged from the apartment building, however, he had not needed the glasses to identify the man's forward-leaning walk or the worn, jagged features glimpsed in the light from the lobby as the door drifted shut behind him. His memory had not trained as well as Macklin's, but concentration was an acquired skill, and his study of the photos and written description had been thorough.

It was cold in the car. He had opened his window all the way to keep the windshield and his glasses from clouding, and his topcoat, purchased for twenty francs in a Paris thrift shop, was inadequate for autumn nights in Michigan. He buttoned the collar around his fleshy neck, removed a brown jersey glove to feed himself another capsule from the bottle he had carried from his hotel room, and hurriedly put the glove back on before sipping from the plastic water bottle. He drank only enough to help down the capsule. As it was, his bladder no longer accommodated itself to long waits in enclosed spaces.

Screwing the cap back on the bottle, he set it on the floor and made himself comfortable out of the draft from the window. He was confident the noise of an engine starting or a car door slamming would awaken him out of his customarily light slumber.

He always did his watching from the backseat on the passenger side, where curious eyes never wandered. Nosy neighbors and passersby always looked behind the wheel. People did the same things the same way every time. It was infuriating and exhilarating.

Chapter Sixteen

"**H**ave you an appointment?"

From behind her sleek racing number of a desk, the woman in the starched blouse managed to appear to be looking down at the tall bald black man. Pontier showed her his badge folder. She repeated her question.

"He knows I'm coming," he said, putting it away. "I said I'd be in sometime this morning."

"That's not very specific."

"Miss, I've got six homicides on my desk and an officer dying at Wayne County General of wounds received in a holdup at two this morning. I don't have time to be specific."

"It's Mrs." She raised the receiver from the telephone-intercom and spoke into it quietly. Pontier judged her to be approaching middle age, but along an elegant route. She was a handsome woman rather than a beautiful one, with strawberry hair pulled behind her head and an almost Oriental slant to her hazel eyes. She wore a plain gold band on the third finger of her left hand.

She cradled the receiver. "Go right in, Inspector."

He had to walk around the end of the desk to go through the door. It blocked the opening. Inside, a man as tall as Pontier, but very broad in the shoulders and heavy-waisted, was just rising from behind his desk in front of a bulletproof window overlooking the river. His hair was white with streaks of tired red in it and his square granite face held an indoor pallor. His grip when they shook hands was brutal.

"Inspector," greeted the federal man in a pleasant rumbling bass. "It's a pleasure. I've heard a great deal about you."

"The same here." The detective wondered if the director of local FBI operations had been briefed by his people on Pontier the way Pontier had had Sergeant Lovelady brief him on Randall Burlingame. Ostensibly on the same team, law enforcement officials on opposite sides of the federal fence could operate for years within a few blocks of each other, each unaware of the other's existence until necessity changed the rule. "Quite a bottleneck you've got out there," the inspector commented.

"If you mean Mrs. Gabel, I inherited her from three predecessors and so far I haven't even been able to get their home addresses out of her. If you mean the barricade, I was here one week when a nut armed with a .357 mag tore through that door looking for the man who tanked his brother-in-law for mail robbery. I put him down on the sill. One shot from an old-fashioned Police Special."

Pontier looked back the length of the office. "What, eighteen feet?"

"Nineteen and a little. The shape of the room helped. It's like the range in Washington."

"Bullshit, Mr. Director. I stopped playing that game when they stenciled my name on the door."

Burlingame smiled, tugging out his lips slightly. "Where'd I slip up?"

"Nowhere special. I've just got this built-in shit detector."

"Yeah. You and Hemingway. The guy had a Saturday nighter with a broken firing pin. Security nabbed him without a shot. I was at lunch. I'm through flexing my muscles if you are."

"I guess we're just a couple of unliberated males," Pontier said.

"Unregenerate. Unreconstructed." The federal man flipped a hand at the chair on Pontier's side of the desk.

"I don't talk to the federal liaison people much," said the inspector when they were comfortable. "They've all got oral constipation and I hate to see them suffer. But the last time I did, they were all high on this new cooperation between government and local authorities."

"First memo I dictated, when this office was still full of packing cartons."

"So I understand. Imagine my surprise when a routine request from my office for federal wants and warrants on a dead Chinese named Robert Lai drew that whiskered old excuse from this office about the computer being down."

"Brides burn breakfasts, Inspector. And computers go on the blink."

"That noise you hear is my shit detector going off again."

Burlingame took a dilapidated pipe out of the brass ashtray on his desk and ran a finger around inside the bowl. "You said the Chinese is dead?"

"Someone shot him in Westland a couple of nights ago. It was in the papers."

"Mrs. Gabel clips all the crime news from the local papers for me to read every day. I don't remember it."

"The Westland Police held back that he was Chinese. That Vincent Chin thing has got everyone looking for a new yellow peril. He was John Doe'd at the morgue until yesterday. Cops on the Coast had him down as a professional mean mother. Washington must have something."

"You've been reading too many books about the FBI with forewords by J. Edgar Hoover. We don't have every lifetaker in the country on file."

"Who said he was a lifetaker?"

Burlingame blew through the pipe and measured out another inch of smile. "I don't figure a Homicide inspector would pry himself loose from his desk for a knucklebuster. What makes a Westland killing Detroit's red wagon?"

"We think our suspect is the same man who was involved in that flamethrower killing downtown early this week."

"The one in Howard Klegg's building?"

"There's been more than one?"

"Who's your man?"

Pontier grinned appreciatively. Burlingame grunted, put down the pipe, and lifted the receiver off the telephone-intercom. "Louise, have that Robert Lai file sent up? Thanks."

He hung up and looked at his guest, who said: "Peter Macklin."

"Uh-huh." The federal man picked up his pipe. "Our information is Macklin's left Michael Boniface's employ. He doesn't have anything to do with Klegg."

"Hey, I never heard of him before we shoveled that pile of ashes out of the stairwell. Your people gave us Macklin. All we did was feed them the eyewitness descriptions of the man seen entering and leaving the building around the time of the explosion."

"He's just a street soldier. Who would hire out-of-town talent to sweep him up?"

"The same people who crapped out with local talent the first time. If I had the answers I wouldn't be here wondering when you're going to get around to filling and lighting that thing."

Burlingame scowled at the pipe and laid it down a second time. "I'm working on quitting. Macklin in custody?"

"No evidence. I'd have tanked him for CCW except he'd have used the gun and anyway I want something that won't slide off. I had a man on him for about five minutes after we talked but he shook him. He moved out on his wife, no known permanent address. Everything about him says contract."

"How'd you nail him down to begin with?"

"Klegg set it up. See, that's how I know they're together. The old shyster is handling his divorce."

"You might have told me that going in."

"I might have."

The federal man used the pause to ask his secretary again about the file on Robert Lai. "On its way," he said, pegging the receiver. "You were smart not to try and take Macklin armed. He never carries a weapon just for show."

"The sergeant I had with me gets his papers next year. A younger man might have fired the instant Macklin drew, but then all we'd have is another corpse to work with. As for the rest, we aren't in this business to get killed."

"Bet you don't talk like that when Internal Affairs is around."

"Those guys are too far from the street. Only cops who have been there and lived to make inspector know what I'm talking about. And maybe federal agents who have lived to make bureau director," he added.

Burlingame changed the subject. "Charles Maggiore wouldn't mind sending flowers to Macklin's funeral, but he's bracing up for a tax beef and awaiting trial on six counts of smuggling guns to South America. He hasn't had time."

"How much time does it take to make a phone call? But I've a feeling you've ruled him out anyway."

Someone tapped on the door. At Burlingame's invitation the handsome secretary entered, handed him a plain gray cardboard folder, and left, her high heels whispering on the thick tough government carpet. The door snicked shut behind her.

Pontier said, "That's it?"

"What did you expect, a big red seal stamped TOP SECRET?"

"Well, yes, now you mention it."

"Everything in this building is top secret. It doesn't have to be marked."

"Including Mrs. Gabel?"

"Her especially. You want to look at this stuff or hunt pussy?"

He had the folder open and its contents spread on the desk. Pontier got out of his chair and came around to Burlingame's side. The pages were of the same heavy stock that had come pasted to the back of Macklin's picture, typewritten in very black ink with wide margins. Seeing them reminded the inspector of something.

"Say, is that true about Hoover and the margins?"

"Yeah. He liked them nice and wide. One time he wrote 'Watch the borders' on a report that crowded them. An aide misunderstood and dispatched special task forces to both the Mexican and Canadian borders."

"Jesus, he must have been fun to work for."

"He was a son of a bitch. But he took a boondoggle left over from the Coolidge Administration and built it into one of the finest law enforcement organizations in the world. People forget that sometimes. Stop me when you see something you like." He was shuffling through a stack of eight-by-ten glossy black-and-white prints.

Several of them showed a young Oriental dressed in an open-necked shirt and dark slacks getting off an airplane ramp carrying a gym bag. It was Robert Lai, a/k/a Chih Ming Shang. Another set recorded a greeting in the airport between Lai and a thin white man with long sideburns and what looked like a garishly bright tie erupting out of his Oxford collar. Pontier stopped Burlingame. "Who's he?"

"We're still running him down." He resumed shuffling.

The pictures appeared to be in sequence: Lai and the thin man getting into a taxi in front of the terminal, getting out of the cab before a building Pontier recognized, the two going inside. Lai held on to his bag. The last group didn't include him at all, but the thin man and a much larger, broader senior built along Burlingame's lines but even bulkier through the chest and shoulders. These had been zoom-shot through the building's open front door.

"You know the wrestler?" Pontier asked.

"If you go by his passports you can call him whatever you want and chances are he's used the name. The one he keeps coming back to is Vasily Andreivich Kurof. He's a Russian national with visitor's status in this country. He was a major in the Red Army with ambitions to the Politburo until the present faction ousted him along with thirty-six others. The other thirty-five went to Labianka Prison. He defected here, probably with CIA help, and his request for asylum is still pending with the State Department. We've had him under surveillance since he got here."

"What is he, some kind of double agent?"

"We don't know. There's a good chance his ouster was just window dressing to burrow him in here. He's shrewd as hell. This is as much activity as we've picked up on him in the year and a half he's been in the area."

"I know that building," Pontier said.

"It's a former health club on Larned with the second floor converted to private apartments. He lives there. We suspect he owns it through intermediaries, which is illegal for an alien with nonresident status, but that's one for Immigration. He's up to something. These were taken yesterday morning." The federal man unwound the string from an interoffice brown envelope he had taken from a drawer and tipped another sheaf of photographs out onto the desk.

At first they appeared to be duplicates of the airport shots Pontier had already seen, but then he noticed that the man with the sideburns and bright necktie was accompanied by the Russian Kurof and that Robert Lai was not present. In his place stood a much older man in a cheap topcoat and one of those hats Swiss yodelers wore in cartoons, with a feather in the band. Round-lensed spectacles made blank cutouts of his eyes in the light of the concourse.

"He's another new player we don't have any stats for," Burlingame said. "According to the airplane manifest he's traveling under the name I. Wanze and changed planes for Detroit in New York after an overseas flight from London. Customs is all bollixed up as usual but we're waiting on a call to them and a Telex to the CIA in Maryland. Those James Bond types take their own sweet time getting back to us on everything. There's another appropriations battle going on in Congress and they take everything personally."

Pontier said, "He doesn't look German."

"He looks like a Ukrainian potato-digger on vacation. For all we know he could be the next premier of the U.S.S.R."

"What's this got to do with Macklin?"

"Until you walked in here I didn't know it had anything to do with him." Burlingame was again probing absentmindedly inside his pipe. "But if it does, you better tell your friends in the morgue to move over."

Chapter Seventeen

The inspector resumed his seat while Burlingame sorted the photographs and information into their proper containers. The printed matter on Lai was just a copy of the information the police in Los Angeles had sent Sergeant Lovelady. "What makes Macklin so special?" Pontier asked.

"You're Homicide. Which killers are the easiest to catch?"

"The family kind. Husbands and sisters and brothers-in-law that get into an argument about which TV show to watch and wind up putting a hole through their loved ones. They're sitting there with the gun when the uniforms show. After that there's the fancy kind of kill that somebody gussied up to look like something else. The job looks too easy. The hardest would be the ones that walk up to a complete stranger on a street corner and clobber him and walk away."

"There's one harder," said Burlingame. "The pro who stalks his man and pops him without music. He leaves the body where it fell and loses the weapon and goes home to drink Stroh's and watch the Lions."

"They're just instruments, though. No faces. Then you look for the guy that paid them. Our information says Macklin's solo now."

"Yeah, but he put in his time as an instrument and he took his savvy with him when he left. You read a lot of shit about these guys being psychopaths with nightmares who keep prostitutes on retainer to whip them for their sins. There are some like that, I guess, but they burn out fast. These lifers punch in and out five days a week and take two weeks off for vacation in January. It's just a job and a damn dull one, to them anyway. Fuck conscience. You ever visit a sewage disposal plant?''

Pontier hesitated. ''About thirty years ago, on a field trip with my high school conservation class. What's—''

''You talk to any of the workers?''

''I guess. Yeah, one.''

''You remember what he said when you asked him how he stood the smell?''

After a moment the inspector smiled. ''He said, 'What smell?' ''

Burlingame sat back and charged the pipe finally from a tattered pouch. He struck a wooden kitchen match on the sole of his shoe and held it up, waiting for the sulfur to burn off. ''I guess you know about Macklin and us last August,'' he said, watching it. ''Among federal and local cops it's got to be the worst-kept secret since Hiroshima.''

''I was going to ask you about that.''

''Our statistics people predicted a two-point-five percent casualty rate among innocent passengers aboard that boat. We allowed for five percent. That's twenty to forty bystanders dead or wounded. That's if he was successful, and I won't quote you the odds they gave us on that. Otherwise it was a hundred-percent dead loss. We got four nervous breakdowns and a plumbing contractor with a shattered kneecap. Armed with just a .38 revolver and a skindiver's knife, Macklin took on seven terrorists holding assault rifles and semiautomatic pistols and brought the boat in safely.'' He finished lighting the tobacco and shook out the match. ''That's what makes him so special.''

Pontier watched the smoke uncoiling from the ashtray. ''You talk about him like some hero-struck kid. He's a paid murderer.''

'' 'Murderer' is a hell of an emotional word for a Homicide inspector to be using,'' Burlingame said. ''It sounds too white-collar for a guy like Macklin anyway. He's just a plain old killer, like Fred's a carpenter and Bill's an auto mechanic. He's no Captain Indestructo. If he had any ambition, he wouldn't still be doing what he does. He'd be running video games in Harper Woods or selling stolen furs in Grosse Pointe. He's mostly nerves and reflexes. He's got the brains of a turtle. You ever try to kill a turtle?"

"I'm not out to kill anyone. I'm just trying to hold the line and not having a hell of a lot of success. What started out as a simple killing downtown is getting to look like a shooting script for Roger Moore. I don't even know who has jurisdiction."

"Join the club. With Kurof and this potato-digger involved it could be CIA's scooter, only they have no authority inside the United States. The book says. Immigration and the Secretary of State each get a slice and every day there's a new alphabet soup agency to deal with out of Washington. Just for now let's say Macklin is yours and we'll worry about the foreign talent. I'd like to have a liaison man in your office to see we don't stumble over each other."

"Uh-uh. No spies. I'll keep an open line into this office. We'll both use it."

Burlingame's lips made popping noises on the stem of his pipe. The inspector thought he looked not at all like a fattish Sherlock Holmes. Finally the federal man rose and thrust out a hand.

"You ever get tired of working for the city," he said.

Pontier grasped the hand. "No thanks. I like having just one boss. I couldn't handle the whole Constitution."

"Thanks for coming down, Inspector."

"Chewing gum," said Pontier.

"What?"

He indicated the pipe. "It'll help keep your mind off that. It's how my brother quit."

"I'd try it, only it's hard to hold a field agent's attention while you're snapping your spearmint."

"Just a suggestion."

The detective left. Burlingame waited a full minute, then got on the intercom and asked Louise Gabel to put through a call to another office in the building. When a man's voice came on the line he said, "Phil, who's our man in Detroit Homicide?"

"Second." Keys rattled on Phil's end. "Lester Flood, detective first grade. Lieutenant's name is Gritch."

"Get him a transfer onto Inspector George Pontier's detail." The bureau chief spelled the name. "Oh, and Phil? Send someone out for a pack of chewing gum, will you?"

"Sugarless or what?"

"Surprise me." He hung up and knocked his pipe out on the edge of the ashtray.

Chapter Eighteen

The car was a three-year-old Plymouth with a peeling vinyl top and Bondo'd patches showing flat and sullen around its fenders and at the corners of doors because they didn't reflect light like the rest of the car's blue finish. It stood alone in a row of empty diagonal spaces at the end of the lot farthest from the doors of the covered shopping mall.

Macklin, standing on the other side of the small square painted plywood building where keys were made in the center of the lot, had been watching the car since its arrival ten minutes before. Its driver was still seated behind the wheel and from where he was standing the other seats appeared empty.

"There you go, sir. That'll be five-twenty." The bearded young man behind the open window in the building handed Macklin back his keys and five colorful copies stamped out of sheet metal.

Macklin thanked him, paid for the keys, and pocketed them. He hadn't needed copies. Two of the originals he had handed the young man belonged to the ignition and trunk of his Cougar, a third opened the front door of the house he had shared with Donna for most of their married life, and of the others, one fit his apartment and the last was a mystery. It had been on his ring so long he had forgotten its purpose. The transaction was just a stall to give him time to study the car and its occupant without drawing notice. With his sport coat over his right arm he crossed directly to the car and opened the door on the passenger side and got in.

Treat, who had been watching his approach, ignored the gun concealed under the checked coat and watched his guest's face. Outside of his home, the gun dealer's shoe-shaped face looked old and drawn and there were burst vessels in his divided nose. The inside of the car smelled sharply of gun lubricant.

"This stinks," he said.

"Open the window."

"I mean getting up and getting out. We could of done this back at my place in Taylor."

"You know I don't go to a place twice if I can help it," Macklin said. "Never when I'm on the stick."

"Yeah, well, it's going to cost you. I had to cancel a piano lesson. The kid's father's my dentist and I got a molar needs yanking."

"What'd you bring me?"

"You said you didn't want a .38."

"It's getting to be like my thumbprint."

"In the trunk."

"Okay, let's have a look."

"Put up that thing first," Treat said. "I know how little trigger pull it takes and I don't want to wear any lead just because you slipped getting out."

Macklin holstered the Smith & Wesson and they climbed out and went around to the trunk. He tucked in the tail of his shirt, which he had been wearing outside his pants to cover the holster, and put on the coat while his companion unlocked and flung up the lid. Treat peeled back the foam rubber pad that concealed the cavity where the spare tire belonged. It glittered with pistols and revolvers and knocked-down rifles wrapped in glassine and pink naval jelly.

"What if you get a flat?"

"I call Triple-A like any good member." The dealer

unwrapped a shiny square pistol, shielding it with his body from the populated end of the parking lot. It was the 10-millimeter semiautomatic he had showed Macklin earlier. The killer swore.

"Cops'll just follow the ejected shells back to me."

"How? The model's experimental. They'll be a week just arguing over is it a 9-millimeter or a .38. By then it should be rusting in the river with all the other hardware. This one's a prototype. Doesn't even have a serial number."

"I don't like automatics."

"You said. But revolvers only come in a few realistic calibers. Thirty-twos don't have the stopping power and .44s are more iron than you like to lug around. You don't like mags."

"Using a magnum on just a man is like putting five stamps on a letter that only needs one," Macklin said. "I hate wasting firepower."

Treat opened his dark palm in the direction of the 10-millimeter.

"How much?" Macklin asked.

"For you, a grand."

"I don't have a grand on me. If I did I wouldn't trade it for this."

"You're hot. You can't go back to your place and you can't tap your bank. But you'd have walking-around money, a pro like you."

"You get five hundred, same as before."

"Gimme the gun."

"Five-fifty, and you toss in a case of ammo."

"Eight," Treat said. "Box of a hundred."

"Six and I don't put a hole in you right here."

"Gun ain't loaded."

"I'm wearing one that is."

The dealer grinned. "We did this before. I didn't have to tell you then, but I'll tell you now. I got a file of test-fired bullets from every gun I've sold, all labeled as to who bought them. A friend's holding them along with a note telling him where to send them if he don't hear from me once a week."

"That old snore."

"Hey, I deal to killers. I sold you three pieces in the last two years. That's three counts anyway. Unless you missed once."

"Six-fifty. Box of a hundred."

"Seven and I make it a case."

"I needed a case I'd be in some other business," Macklin said.

"Why'd you ask for one before?"

"Thrill of the deal."

The exchange was made.

"Mister, would you put in a quarter?"

The old man, standing on the covered sidewalk fronting the mall, started and looked over the top of his glasses at the little girl in jeans and a Smurf sweatshirt straddling the coin-operated hobby horse. She had bright red hair and blue eyes and freckles the size of dimes. He returned her smile and folded his chins on his chest while he fished among the keys and change in his pants pocket. The afternoon was almost balmy and he had left his coat in the car. His green sweater and the feathered hat were protection enough.

The quarter clanked inside the machine and the horse started undulating. "Thanks, mister."

"You're welcome."

When he returned his gaze to the other end of the lot, the gray-haired man was standing alone beside the scuffed blue car. The old man looked around quickly and spotted Macklin coming up the next aisle to where his silver car was parked. He smiled again at the little girl and stepped off the curb and into his rental parked in front.

Mantis was an expert at following people. Back home it had been his specialty for years before he had stepped up into what the Americans called the K unit. It had been said of him that he could track a grain of sand in a duststorm, and he was vain enough to enjoy the myth, but in truth it was very simple business. Most tail men tried too hard to be inconspicuous, scuttling from cover to cover on foot and speeding up and slowing down and passing their subjects behind the wheel in the belief that this was preferable to holding a steady pace. He had known one who kept a collection of hats and caps in the backseat of his car so that he could keep changing them, imagining that this would distract his quarry from the fact that the same car was still behind him after several miles. Mantis had helped bury the man after he was found parked in a ditch with a bullet hole in his temple and an American baseball cap on the back of his head. The trick was to drive a nondescript vehicle and give your man some distance and maintain the gap.

He followed Macklin down East Jefferson and turned right onto the Belle Isle Bridge a block and a half behind him. The sun was bright and struck sparks off the surface of the Detroit River. Upstream a pair of sailboats skated the water like bright moths around a long rust-colored ore carrier hog-nosing its way down from Lake Superior. The old man's tires whistled on the bridge's steel ribs.

He parked in a lot several spaces down from the Cougar, pulling in just as Macklin alighted from the driver's side. Mantis stayed where he was while his man strolled down the footpath leading away from the big marble fountain where most of the island's visitors congregated. He knew Macklin would be coming back to his car, and he knew what he had come to the island to do. Mantis would have done the same thing if he had a used gun to dispose of.

There was a pay telephone at one corner of the lot, within sight of both cars. The old man got out and fed it and dialed Mr. Brown's number.

"I am just calling to determine that plans have not changed with regard to the package," he said when the other's smoothly lathed voice came on the wire.

"They're the same. You've found him?"

"Through the King woman. I am watching his car now."

"What's he doing?"

"Admiring the river, I suspect. Dropping things into it."

The pause on Brown's end asked a question.

"Not bodies," the old man assured him. "He moves no faster than I. I think I like him."

"Don't become too attached."

"I have liked others. It has never interfered."

"When can you act?"

"Sooner than I would like. He appears to be a man of no habits at all. I have been following him for a day and he has done nothing the same way twice or in the same place. It is all very challenging and I should like to pursue the matter for a month but for the time factor. There have been opportunities. I think that I will use the next one that presents itself."

"Very good. You'll call me if you need anything."

"I will call when it is done."

He pegged the receiver, inspected the coin return and found it empty, sighed, and went back to the Oldsmobile. Removing the Walther from the glove compartment, he checked the load and laid it on the seat beside him. After shadowing Macklin to his motel the night before, he had waited until the light had gone off in Macklin's room, then gone back to his own hotel to retrieve the pistol. It felt good next to his thigh, like an erection in his younger days.

Chapter Nineteen

Moira King left the recording booth for coffee and a cigarette. The afternoon session had not gone well, and the pressure of the earphones had given her a headache.

She found the small employee lounge deserted and carried her Styrofoam cup of coffee from the machine to the first cafeteria table, sitting with her back to the open door. The room smelled of coffee and cheap floor wax. It was an improvement over all those makeshift studio bedrooms she had performed in with their bitter marijuana stench and the cloying odor of human biology at its basest.

The telephone office was a good place to work. She could wear what she wanted—today it was corduroy slacks and a sleeveless blue cotton blouse, no tight garter belt or slippery step-ins or net stockings that felt like barbed wire on her toes after a full day's shooting on five-inch heels—and she always learned something from the messages she recorded for callers seeking information on the weather or books available at the library or the fishing around Michigan or any of the half a hundred other topics the telephone company kept tabs on for its subscribers. She had a good speaking voice, no thanks to the minimal dialogue provided by the scriptwriters for her films, and she sometimes picked up extra money weekends recording books and magazines for the blind. If any of her employers had seen her previous work, none made mention of it, probably because none wanted it known he sought such entertainment.

But today she had found herself unable to concentrate on the words she was reading. There had been many retakes, until she grew sick of saying the same things over and over and started making mistakes out of irritation. Thinking got in the way. Retakes were not her strong suit. They were practically unknown in her former profession, whose low budgets didn't allow for make-goods, and in which it was next to impossible to make the sort of error that would require one in the first place. Sex was difficult to get wrong.

That thought reminded her of last night. It had been very different with Macklin. She wasn't sure why. She was hardly an adventuress anymore and doubted that she was aroused by what he did for a living, although she had known women who talked about grisly murders they had read about in the papers and who wondered aloud what it would be like to go to bed with the culprits. Nor was it that he was particularly good. His foreplay consisted of fumbling for her breasts and then her vagina, after which he got down to business and was through in under five minutes. But there was an animalistic simplicity about his lovemaking that she had not known in the false prolonged titillation under the strobes or with a marathon man like Roy or with the panting, French-kissing boys she had gone into backseats with in high school. He was a simple needs-and-fulfillment man, knew how to go about it, and yet somehow managed to seem to remain aware of her throughout the act.

It wasn't love, she decided. She didn't even like the man. He frightened her at least as much as Roy. But if she were to plan sex with a man for the first time in months, it would be with someone who wouldn't forget she was there.

"Penny for 'em, Slick."

She looked up quickly from the inside of her empty cup. Roy was just swinging a leg cowboy-fashion over the bench facing hers on the other side of the table. He had on his favorite navy peacoat, open over bare chest, and his thick wheat-colored hair broke in twin wings over his forehead the way she remembered watching him train it to do after he had seen James Cagney in *Angels with Dirty Faces*. He had Cagney's sneering grin and Robert Mitchum's sleepy lids and one of the things that had always unnerved her was that she never knew how much of it was him and how much the old movies he was always watching on afternoon television.

"How'd you get in here?" She almost shrieked it. She glanced around quickly. They were alone in the room, but she forced her voice down anyway. "Only authorized personnel are allowed in this part of the building."

"Yeah, but there ain't no guards. Them signs scared the living shit out of me but I got over my scared and here I am. Thought you'd be glad to see me."

"I told you to leave me alone."

He got out his oversize pocketknife, making a face as he pried it loose from the pocket of his tight jeans, and unfolded the big curved blade, then folded it again and pulled it out again, playing with it. "I see you had a guest last night. He stayed a lick."

His fifth-grade dropout way of talking had always annoyed her. He had studied a year at Penn State before his parents' money ran out. He saw her looking at the knife and grinned wider.

"She's brand-new and a little stiff. They took away my good one when they busted me. Had that one so loose I could flip her open by the blade. Man, wasn't that nigger surprised in that parking lot, though."

"Why do you have it? Nobody carries pocketknives anymore."

"That's what happened to this country. Guys stopped carrying jackknives. Then Kennedy got shot and all hell broke loose. Who's your new boyfriend? Kind of old, ain't he?"

"Why are you watching my apartment?"

"Bet he don't get it up but once a week. Me, I'm hard all the time. This lady shrink was going to write a paper on me in Ypsi. Said I was a psycho-physical phenomenon." He stumbled over the syllables. "Aw, but then the rest of the shrinks got together and turned me loose. She wouldn't of been too bad if there was a paper bag handy. Nice high tits. How's yours, Slick? They still nice and high?" He looked.

"I'll call security."

"I'll wait." He drew her empty cup over to his side of the table and started working at it with the knife, carving curved slices out of the side.

She didn't move. "I'll lose my job."

"There's jobs and jobs. You put on a couple of pounds, use that body makeup, you'll do okay. Look at Linda Lovelace. Bowwow."

"I'm out of that, I told you. I made my decision when you killed that man. Did I tell you I wasn't surprised? What surprised me was I stayed long enough to see you do it."

"You wasn't there."

"I didn't mean it literally."

"Who's your boyfriend?"

"I don't have boyfriends. I'm not a cheerleader."

"Maybe I find out myself." He had finished cutting up the cup and was subdividing the pieces, the edge of the blade clicking on the table's metal top.

"Why are you doing this?"

"You got to use a knife now and again or you're always sharpening it."

"You know what I mean."

"We're just talking. I like to talk. So do you. Didn't matter what we was doing, you just went on jabbering right through it. Remember? It's the one time I wanted you to shut up."

"My break's over." She rose.

A hand shot out and closed tightly on her wrist. The other held the knife with its butt on the table and the blade pointing up. "Dump Grandpa, Slick."

"You're cutting off my circulation." But she made no attempt to pull free.

"There's better ways."

"Miss King?"

They looked at the doorway. A middle-aged man with gray hair and a moustache and glasses stood in it. He had a hearing aid clipped to the handkerchief pocket of his blue suit with a wire leading to a plug in his right ear.

"I'm just going back, Mr. Turner." She was watching Roy now, who smiled and let go of her wrist. He had folded the knife one-handed and put it away.

Mr. Turner looked at him for the first time. "Sir, are you an employee? If not I'm afraid I'll have to ask you to leave."

Roy opened his mouth and closed it several times without making a sound.

"I'm sorry?" Mr. Turner twisted the dial on the hearing aid.

Roy got up and leaned forward and cupped his hands around his mouth, opening it wide. Nothing came out. Turner unclipped the instrument and frowned at it, tapping the case.

"Roy—" Moira said.

The man in the suit caught on then. He returned the device to the outside of his pocket. "I see. Very funny. Is this man a friend of yours, Miss King?"

"I was just giving him directions to the billing department."

"You the guy in charge?" Roy said.

"I'm the supervisor on this shift."

"I got a bill needs adjusting. You guys stuck me with two long-distance calls I didn't make. I figure you're making up for all them other phone companies taking away your business."

"I'm sure it was an oversight. If you'll—"

"Oversight hell!" He was shouting. His face was white, the skin drawn tight. "You fuckers think you got us all by the balls. How you like I cut off that flash necktie and shove it up your ass?" His hand went to his pocket.

Turner looked away. "You'll find that department on the ground floor. Miss King?"

She hesitated, watching Roy. His hand was out of his pocket now, empty. His color was normal again. She turned toward the doorway.

Roy said, "I mean it, Slick. Old fart stays he could get hurt."

She went out past the man in the suit without turning around.

"I'll show you to the right elevator," Turner said. "Mr.—?"

"Bates." The young man walked out in front of him. "Norman."

Chapter Twenty

Judge Flutter closed the file, handed it to his bailiff, a retired black Wayne County Sheriff's deputy with a smudge of purple ink on the left side of his nose, and folded his big slow hands on the desk in front of him. "Very equitable. I think we can set the date for a final hearing. Does November the eighth meet with any strong objections? It's a Thursday."

Howard Klegg, seated at one corner of the desk with his long thin legs crossed, glanced at Macklin, who nodded. He raised his eyebrows at Gerald Goldstick, sitting next to Donna Macklin at the other corner. The young lawyer was studying a pocket calendar card. Klegg distrusted people who carried them. They always knew exactly where they would be on any given date three months in advance. It suggested an arrogant faith in their longevity.

"Friday's better," Goldstick said, looking up.

"This court doesn't sit Fridays," the judge explained.

"Thursday then."

Little twerp had Thursday clear all along, thought Klegg.

The lawyers shook Flutter's hand and the four left. In the hallway outside chambers, Macklin trotted ahead of Klegg to catch his wife. Goldstick hesitated, but Donna touched two fingers to his forearm and he went on ahead. Klegg, lagging along behind, caught some of the conversation as the pair walked.

"Seen Roger lately?" Macklin asked.

"No. I called Lonnie Kimball's. He moved out yesterday. Lonnie didn't know where."

"That stinks."

"What do you want me to do, put a detective on him?"

"Call the cops. He's still a minor."

"He'd just run away again. If what you said to him did any good, that might be enough to change his mind back the other way."

"It didn't do any good," he said. "I just wasted time."

"You don't know that."

"I know Roger."

"Like hell you do. If you knew him, we wouldn't have this problem. You were never home."

"You were, though. All you had to do was count the empties to see that."

They walked along for a few yards without saying anything. "Why didn't you call Klegg when you found out he left the apartment?" he demanded.

"I'm through running to you."

"When did this happen?"

"I'm a grown woman. I don't have to tell my soon-to-be ex-husband when I'm going to the toilet."

He looked down the hall at Goldstick, who was standing before the floor directory with his hands folded in front of him on the handle of his briefcase. "Yeah." Macklin fell back.

"What was all that about?" asked Klegg, drawing abreast.

"Not much. My wife's sleeping with her attorney."

"It sounded serious."

"With her it never was a lot of laughs."

The old lawyer glanced sideways at Macklin, wondering if he was developing a sense of humor.

"Roger Macklin," Gordy announced.

Charles Maggiore, bench-pressing on the Nautilus in his

basement gym, paused with the bar across his naked chest.
"On the phone?"

"On the stoop."

"Shit." He resumed pressing.

"I should tell him scram?"

"Give me a couple of minutes, then chase him in."

The big manservant nodded once and turned around and
started up the stairs. The room seemed much larger in his
absence.

Maggiore did two more reps and locked the bar in place.
Getting up from the bench, he hooked a towel off the
padded exercise horse and used it on his face and chest,
avoiding his reflection in the bank of mirrors mounted across
from him. That alone would have been enough to sour his
mood if it were any brighter. Normally he was a man who
liked mirrors, or anything else with a surface shiny enough
to show him his good build and careful tan and Beach Boy
good looks, so youthful for a man in his fifties. But of late all
those hours locked up with his lawyers and accountants had
kept him from his sunlamps and his exercise and he was
unwilling to face the ravages of neglect. He valued what time
he could steal to slow them down.

He finished toweling off and slid into a terry robe with a
padded left shoulder to balance the hump on his right just as
Peter Macklin's boy came down the stairs. Roger was wearing a faded blue plaid workshirt open over a black T-shirt
and a pair of jeans at least a size too large for him around the
waist. His tightened belt drew pleats in the worn material
and his bare bony ankles made his feet look big in soiled
track shoes. His young face was lined under the fluorescent
lights in the ceiling.

"Thanks for seeing me, Mr. Maggiore." He held out a
skeletal hand.

The Sicilian, a gang-war veteran who shared Roger's
father's distrust of the gesture, let go quickly. "What can I do

for you, son? I'm meeting the bean-counters again upstairs in twenty minutes."

"I was just wondering if you had anything for me yet."

"Not yet. I said I'd call."

"See, that's another reason I came. I'm not at that number anymore. I got an attic room in a place off Gratiot, doing fix-up work for the old lady that lives there. No bathroom or telephone."

"Need money?"

"Well, I want to earn it."

Maggiore smiled and clapped Roger's shoulder. "Let's go upstairs."

In the library the Sicilian slid out the top drawer of the desk and lifted out a triple-decker checkbook. Writing: "Couple of hundred see you through?"

"This a loan, right?"

"Let's call it an advance against your first job."

"I'm ready to work, Mr. Maggiore. My nerves are settling down."

"Seen your father lately?" He signed the check and tore it free.

"Other day." Roger reached for it, but Maggiore held it back, looking at him.

"You didn't tell him anything."

"You mean about working for you? Well, yeah, but he already knew, sort of. Ma told him."

"You told your *mother*?"

"She guessed it. She's sharp that way. See, she's a lush, and sometimes I can get away with—well, a lot. Then other times—"

"I can't believe you told your mother you're going into the killing business."

Roger shrugged, eyeing the check.

Maggiore sat back, absentmindedly folding the check lengthwise and stroking it between two fingers. Finally he flicked it out. When the boy's fingers closed on it he held on.

"What'd your father say?"

"Tried to scare me out of it. Gave me the royal tour of the morgue." He tried a grin. "Hell, I guess he don't know I have worse dreams. Snakes and spiders, my dick falling off. They're going away now, though," he added quickly.

"I mean did he say anything about me."

"He called you a son of a bitch."

"Anything else?"

He shook his head. "Hey, are you afraid of him?"

Maggiore's other hand made a short, swift arc. Roger howled and jerked back the hand with which he'd been holding the check. The fountain pen the Sicilian had used to sign it stuck out of the back, its point half buried in the flesh. He pulled it out and clapped his other hand over the pumping blood.

"I was younger than you when I killed my first man," said the Sicilian. "Caved in his skull with a rock. You come back to me after you've done that and tell me about being afraid."

Gordy filled the open doorway.

"Treasury men outside," he announced. "Say they got a warrant to search the place."

Maggiore said shit. "You see it?"

"Just the envelope."

"Read it."

"Fine print?"

"The watermark, everything. Get me two minutes."

The big man paused, looking from his employer to the boy holding on to his right hand with his left. Then he left the room. Maggiore pushed the check closer to Roger's side of the desk.

"Think you could remember a telephone number without writing it down?"

Roger sucked at the wound. "I guess."

"Because if you can't and you do and it gets found on you, the medical examiner's going to wonder where that mark on your hand came from."

"I'll remember it."

Maggiore told him the number. Roger repeated it twice.

"Call between six and six-ten any night, give your name. If there's no answer, it means there's nothing for you. Otherwise listen to the instructions."

"Okay."

Maggiore stood, adjusting the tie of his robe. "Use the back way out, past the pool."

Roger turned to leave. The other called him back.

"Forgot your check."

The boy picked it up.

"You better get that hand looked at. Blood poisoning's nothing to fool with."

Randall Burlingame placed a thin sheaf of neatly typewritten sheets on Louise Gabel's desk. He had his topcoat folded over one arm.

"Get these out tomorrow, okay? They're expense vouchers, and Washington likes them nice and slow."

She nodded and glanced coolly out the window on the Detroit side of the outer office. "It could rain. You ought to wear a hat."

"I stopped doing that the day Hoover died. He had a thing about fedoras in public at all times. Thought the head was another erogenous zone."

"You catch pneumonia, that'll show him."

"How long have you been mothering me, Louise?"

"How long have I been your secretary?"

A young man hurried in from the hall carrying a brown interdepartmental envelope. He had on a maroon three-piece suit and wore his sandy hair razor-cut around the ears. His ID was attached to his handkerchief pocket by the regulation blue plastic clothespin. The bureau director, who had lost his and used a paper clip, thought he looked like a cross between Robert Stack and Efrem Zimbalist, Jr. "Mr.

Burlingame, I'm glad I caught you before you went to lunch."

"What is it, Fieldhouse?"

The young man smiled broadly. "I'm surprised you remember me, sir."

"I read your ID. What can't wait?"

"This just got in over the Telex from Washington." Fieldhouse handed him the envelope. "I knew you'd want to see it right away. It's on that man Intertrap operatives photographed with the Chinese and with Vasily Kurof. The one with the sideburns."

Burlingame lifted the flap and read the printout. When he was finished, he looked at the young agent.

"Who else has seen this?"

"No one, sir. I realize I should have gone to my supervisor—"

"Who's your supervisor?"

"Reed Wallace, sir. Records and Research."

"Mrs. Gabel, have Mr. Fieldhouse transferred to the director's staff." To the agent: "That is, if you don't object."

"No, sir!"

Burlingame retied the string on the envelope. "You've just reported to your supervisor. No need to bother Mr. Wallace with it. Or anyone else."

"Yes, sir."

The director looked at the agent's hair. "Grow that out a little on the sides, can you? You look like a G-man."

Chapter Twenty-one

The farm was overgrown with quackgrass and timothy and the ugly thistled weeds that grew only where land had been tilled and then left to the wild. The barn had fallen in, and where the house had stood, a charred foundation and an exposed dirt cellar scarred a lawn gone over to poison ivy and wild wheat. Even the chimney bricks had been carried off by scavengers. Only the barbed wire enclosing the sixty acres was new, strung taut and stapled to creosoted cedar posts driven four feet into the earth and rising another four feet above, straight as rifle cartridges placed at fifteen-foot intervals.

Macklin used his key on the padlock securing the gate, swung it out, and got back into his car to baby it over the rutted remains of the driveway, parking it behind a spray of young box elders growing out of the cistern. Then he walked back and closed the gate and locked it.

The air was brisk and high cirrus clouds drifted overhead, casting feathery shadows that moved swiftly along the ground. Macklin had shed his sport coat in favor of a new waist-length fifty-percent wool red-and-black-checked fall jacket. The feel and smell of it reminded him favorably of hunting holidays with his father before the bad times came and made them strangers. On his way past the ruins of the house he unholstered the 10-millimeter, fished the fully loaded magazine out of a slash pocket, blew into it to dislodge lint, and heeled it into the gun's hollow handle. Even with the clip in place it felt incredibly light.

The land was his, or rather his and the bank's, secured with a ten-thousand-dollar down payment to the widow of a Hamtramck numbers king who had bought it as retirement property before a sore loser filled him full of .32 slugs in lieu of debts outstanding. Macklin could have purchased it outright from the hundred thousand he had gotten for the Boblo job, but large cash deals attracted too much notice and the investment in mortgage payments and land taxes was as good a way of laundering capital gains as any accountant could arrange. It was located thirty miles west of Detroit and deeded under a fictitious name, and it was flanked by a Metropark that was closed for the season and a much larger commercial farm whose owner added to his millions by agreeing not to plant crops on the federal government's surplus list. Macklin had no neighbors to worry about.

He had no plans to retire or take up farming. Target ranges were growing rare around an increasingly gun-paranoid city and those that remained boasted more off-duty police officers than a bar across from a precinct house. After Pennsylvania, Michigan led the nation in deer hunters; with the firearms deer season coming up November fifteenth, a few more gunshots in a rural area such as this would pass unnoticed among all the modern-day Daniel Boones tuning up their shooting eyes. Even as he headed out across the overgrown field, carrying a rusted can from the farm's forgotten dump, a report plopped in the distance and echoed sizzlingly across the flat country to prove him right.

When he was far enough away from the road to discourage a good view of the weapon he was using, he selected a pile of rocks cleared from the furrows by some long-dead agrarian and perched the can atop it. Then he paced off sixty feet, turned, set himself, brought the pistol down from a vertical position with his left hand supporting the heel of his right, took quick but careful aim, and squeezed the trigger.

The report was very loud in the open air. The pistol bucked, shooting a little pain back up his wrist. The can clanked and fell over.

His hand tingled. He reversed hands on the gun and shook circulation back into his right, frowning at his target. He favored handguns with heavy frames that absorbed the recoil. This one's kick had thrown him off or else the sight was askew, forcing the trajectory high and to the right so that the bullet just clipped the top of the can instead of plugging it square in the middle as intended. He took aim again from the same distance. Beyond sixty feet an accurate shot was an iffy proposition with the best of handguns; if he were planning anything longer he would have a rifle.

This time he braced himself for the recoil, and the bullet flew straight, rolling the can against an upthrust rock and twanging off stone. He changed his angle and fired a third time, at the can's circular bottom, piercing the center ring dead on. The sight was true. He flicked on the safety and squatted to collect the ejected cartridge cases.

Something split the air above his head with a crack. An instant later came the report, a loud, nasty, shredded pop in the open air. Reflexes took over and he threw himself forward into a crouching run without waiting to see where the shot had come from. Another slapped the space behind him, followed closely by a third. He dived. He hit the ground on his shoulder and then on his chest and then on his back and came to rest on his other shoulder and pulled himself behind the pile of rocks just as another bullet clipped one of the moss-covered chunks of granite. The projectile exploded on contact, spraying tiny buzzing hornets that caught the light like sparks. One of them plucked at his jacket sleeve.

He leaned a shoulder against the pile, breathing heavily and cleaning bits of grass and dirt out of the 10-millimeter's action. When that was done he drew back a little to clear the rocks out of his line of vision. A little scudding patch of smoke drifted with the wind along the fenceline running parallel with the road. He stretched his gun arm over the top of a rock, sighted in on the smoke, and pivoted in the direction from which it had come.

The man was wearing a green top and at first he missed him against the spruce trees lining the road. Then he isolated him, a small pudgy figure under a cartoon hat standing several yards to the left of the burned-out house foundation with legs spread and both hands grasping something that glinted in the sunlight. Macklin depressed the trigger. It moved a tenth of an inch and stopped.

He cursed and slid off the safety. It was another reason he hated semiautomatics. By the time he was ready to fire, his target was moving, with his back to Macklin. He squeezed off three shots.

The pistol was new and smoked too much. He fanned the smoke away impatiently with his free hand. The swollen little figure was gone. Macklin was scanning the landscape for it when an automobile engine started somewhere with a rumble. Tires spun, scratching gravel, and then painted metal flashed through a space between trees, heading east. Macklin listened to the car swishing into the distance and silence.

He didn't get up right away. The trick was as old as turning out the lights and pretending no one was home; one drove off while his partner remained behind, waiting for the quarry to break cover. Macklin made himself comfortable with his back against a slab of limestone and reloaded the 10-millimeter's magazine from the box in his pocket. He ejected the bullet from the chamber and wiped the action with his handkerchief before reassembling.

Another car came down the road, trailing Boy George out an open window. It passed the padlocked gate without slowing and kept moving. A mile off, a tractor started up with a noise like coffee percolating, then died. Someone's dog began barking and went on doing so in a kind of resigned monotony, as if not expecting anyone to pay attention to it. An airplane droned overhead.

Macklin laid the gun to one side and stripped off his jacket. Cold air touched a Y-shaped patch of sweat soaking his shirt between his shoulder blades and down his spine to his belt. He picked up the gun, bunched up the coat, then grunted and put down the coat to rack a shell into the chamber. Then he lifted the coat and drew his legs under him in a crouch and hurled the coat as far as he could.

Its tail and sleeves uncurled in the air, looking at a quick glance like a man running. It completed a lazy twenty-foot arc and flopped to earth.

The airplane droned. The dog barked.

Macklin came out from behind the rocks, still hunched over. After a minute he straightened. No one shot at him. He stood there a while, the pistol in his hand, then went over and retrieved the coat and shrugged into it as he quartered the ground for shell casings. He had already pocketed the ones discarded at the rockpile. He found two quickly where he had been standing to practice but had to look around for a minute before he located the third, perched upright between blades of grass. He tipped them into the pocket with the others and started toward his car.

On the way he swung through the area where his assailant had stood. The county hadn't had rain in a month and the ground was too dry and hard to hold footprints, but a yellow glitter caught his eye and he bent and picked up a shell casing slightly smaller than those he was using. He turned the flanged end to the sun to read the stamped numbers: 7.65. He put the casing in a different pocket from the others and holstered his pistol and walked over to where his car was still parked behind cover and grasped the door handle on the driver's side and pulled.

Five seconds later the doors flew off and balls of yellow-and-red flame uncurled through the Cougar's burst windows from inside.

• • •

"Hell was *that*?" The station attendant jumped at the great hollow *crump* to the west, jerking the hand holding the pump nozzle and splashing gasoline out of the tank onto the asphalt paving and his customer's shoes. He gaped at a column of black smoke smudging the sky where the sun was starting to go down.

The old man scowled down at his shoes and stepped back. "Dynamiting, perhaps?"

"Don't get that much noise and smoke out of the stumps around here."

"Perhaps an accident. Do I also pay for the petrol we are standing in?"

The attendant, short and broad in filthy coveralls, black grease in his gray hair, glanced down at the nozzle and jumped again. He shoved it back into the Oldsmobile's tank. "Knock off a quarter, sorry. Must of been a tank truck turned over. Drivers ain't what they was when I pushed a rig."

A siren started up in the direction of town. The station was on the edge of a country village whose sign described it as a city, two miles from Macklin's property. The old man asked if there were a pay telephone.

"Inside."

There was no one inside the station. He lifted the receiver off the wall unit, slotted a quarter, waited for the fire engine wailing outside to pass, then dialed Mr. Brown's number. When the operator asked for more money for the long distance call, he asked her to reverse the charges.

"That's M-A-N-T-I-S?"

"Yes. Like the insect."

"Brown," said a voice on the other end.

"Collect call from a Mr. Mantis. Will you accept the charges?"

"Yes, I will."

The old man gave the operator time to get off the line, then said, "The package is delivered, Mr. Brown."

"There were no complications?"

"None."

"Excellent. When can you come in to discuss details?"

"As soon as I have wiped my shoes."

He hung up, started out, then went back and retrieved his quarter from the return slot.

Chapter Twenty-two

No one followed Moira home from work.

Once she thought someone was doing it, but after three blocks the car turned off and she didn't see it again. She saw no sign of the silver Cougar she had come to associate with Macklin. But then she had seen nothing of Roy since the incident in the employee lounge. Leaving him with Mr. Turner, she had felt a small thrill of concern and had wanted to warn her supervisor about Roy but could think of no way to do it without going into the details of her past. Fear and disgust with herself had made the second recording session worse than the first, and finally the exasperated technicians had asked her to go home and try again tomorrow. On her way to her locker for her purse, she had passed Mr. Turner in the hall. Her rush of relief as she explained her reasons for leaving early must have puzzled him, but he merely said: "I'm going to put in for more security on this floor. This fellow Bates barging in looks bad."

"Bates?"

"The man who came to complain about his bill. He said his name was Norman Bates."

"Mr. Turner, Norman Bates was the name of the killer in *Psycho*."

"Oh. Maybe I heard him wrong." He played with the dial on his hearing aid. "Anyway, I wish you'd contact me when you find unauthorized parties on this floor."

"I will."

"I rode down with him in the elevator," he said.

"Oh?"

"Strange man."

He had walked off.

Now she was feeling the familiar pressure behind her right eye and left the key in the apartment door while she went into the bathroom to wash down a Valium. The migraines had been troubling her for three years. Once early on, she used one as an excuse to get around a picketer outside a triple-X theater where she had been filming on the second floor. But the picketer, an awful, fat woman of forty, obviously pregnant, with a dirty-faced child hugging each hip and a sign over her shoulder reading DECENCY 1, PORNO 0, had moved to block her path. "That's your guilty conscience, dearie. Virtue is the best aspirin." Walking around her and her brood, Moira had said something back that made the fat woman turn and yell after her, "Fine language in front of two little kids, slut."

Leaning on her hands on the sink, waiting for the Valium to take effect, she studied her face objectively in the mirror. It was a thing she had trained herself to do after that first traumatic exposure to her image on film. No one would think her twenty-two, she decided, looking at the lines connecting her nose and mouth and the puffiness under her eyes that would turn into bags if she didn't do something about them soon. In high school she had read *The Picture of Dorian Gray* and laughed at the notion that the sort of life a person led always showed on his face. But high school was something that had happened to someone else. She couldn't summon up an image of the girl she was then. If her class held a five-year reunion next year, she would avoid it. What have you been doing with yourself, Moira? Oh, popping pills and getting laid for money, the usual stuff.

The drug was working, or else the thought that she had taken it was blunting the pain. She washed off her makeup and patted her face dry with a towel. In the mirror she thought she looked better without the paint, but that was probably the drug. It tended to soften the world's harsh edges like an out-of-focus camera, one of those things with Vaseline on the lens that were already going out of style when she got into movies.

She wondered if Macklin would be coming in tonight, or if he was already there, waiting outside. Thought of him made her stomach quicken. She didn't know why. Yes, she did. She was the queen, he the brute palace guard who came in to service her while the king was away crusading. She had made a film using that plot. What was it called? *The Swordsman.* Only she had been considered too young for the queen's role and had played her lady-in-waiting instead and got two scenes in the hayloft with the royal groom, a graduate student at the University of Detroit who munched on a raw onion during lunch break. Today they would probably ask her to play the queen's mother. Certainly she was too old for sex games, even harmless ones in her head.

Everything she did reminded her of films, she thought disgustedly. She was in danger of becoming a sort of X-rated Norma Desmond. Worse, thinking of that past made her think of Roy and she remembered with exasperation her keys in the apartment door. She went out to get them. They were gone.

The sky purpled, washing the overgrown field below in medium gray. Only a garish smear of bright ragged yellow near the house foundation spoiled the study in subdued hues, that and the rotating lights on top of the trucks and the patrol car parked inside the battered-open gate. Then a tank in the hands of a man wearing a black rubber raincoat and fiberglass helmet whooshed three times and the flames bucked and died, pouring black smoke out of the holes in the burned-out hulk. The man laid down a fourth layer of smothering gas for insurance and stepped forward to peer inside. After a walk around the car he approached an older, white-haired man in similar dress. "Nobody, Chief."

" 'Course not," said the other, around a lump of Skoal wadded under his lower lip. "Deliberate torch job. It didn't crash."

A big man in his thirties wearing the brown uniform and Stetson of the county sheriff's department nodded. "Trundle it into the first lonely spot and torch it to destroy the evidence. As if we ever lifted a set of prints off a car worth going to a judge with. Kids. They see a lot of television."

The trio watched the other firemen hosing down the charred grass around the blackened auto shell.

"Kind of a loud wham for just a match job," suggested the man with the extinguisher.

"Gas tank was about empty, probably. They go up bigger than a full one." The chief spat.

"Gate was locked."

The deputy said, "Picked it."

"Damn polite of them to close it and lock it again after."

"Kids, go figure 'em."

The voices droned, muffled under the gushing nose of the fire hoses and by the uneven stone wall separating them from the man lying on the earthen floor of the open cellar. Weeds grew thickly from the rich, untilled soil, concealing him, their stems and leaves gone brown and brittle after early frosts, and scratching his face where he lay, fully conscious now but unwilling to move lest he discover bones broken or something torn and bleeding inside.

In his shaken condition after the shooting match, Macklin had forgotten to run his car for booby traps until he had the door open. In the instant of remembering he had turned and hurled himself headlong away from the car, paying no heed to the nearness of the deep hole in the ground. The hole had saved his life, for after the filament in the door broke, activating a five-second timer attached to a nitrogelatin charge, the explosion had sprayed flaming gasoline a hundred feet in every direction, missing only the depression where Macklin had landed, knocking himself senseless. He had awakened moments later to the wailing of sirens and drumming of booted feet hitting ground level on the run.

It was dark in the cellar. For a long time he didn't know where he was and wondered groggily if this was death, eternal motionless consciousness in the grave, awareness of his flesh falling away and of blind legless scavengers exploring his cavities. *The worms crawl in, the worms crawl out.* But as his head cleared and the voices above grew separate and more distinct, he remembered the sudden flash of self-preservation and the dive through bottomless empty air and the shocking stop. Eight feet, not counting the six feet covered horizontally on his flight over the foundation wall. He was getting too old for these acrobatics.

"Run the plate," one of the voices was saying. "Check it against the hot sheet from Detroit PD first. That's where they're lifting most of these sports jobs now."

"Who owns this property?" asked another.

"Some Jew from Hamtramck."

"No, he died or something. Someone else bought it a month or so back." Yet a third voice.

"Easy enough to find out who."

In the dark and weeds Macklin waited for the voices and noise to go.

Meaninglessly she ran her hand over the doorknob where she had left the keys hanging. In the long, black moment of realization panic rose in a red arc, but she forced it down and turned with deliberate slowness and walked across the room to the telephone stand, aware of each separate step. She pulled out the drawer and looked at the emptiness inside.

"Look in the cracks, Slick. It's just a little piece. They get lost easy."

She straightened, turned again, more slowly this time. The door drifted shut, pushed by Roy as he came away from the wall behind it. He was wearing his navy coat over smooth bare torso as before. The .25 pistol was so small his long fingers seemed to curl around it twice. He wasn't pointing it at anything, just holding it.

"I was in here before," he said. "I know where you keep everything, your ladies' napkins and everything."

"You're trespassing."

He showed her his Cagney sneer. "That's cowboy movie talk. When's the last time you heard someone getting arrested for trespassing? We're all equal now. Everybody owns everything. We're all like communists. Power to the people. Was a guy in Ypsi thought he was Karl Marx. He had a beard and everything, the works. I learned a lot." He pocketed the gun. "I keep this. You could hurt yourself."

"Get out of here."

He walked around the apartment. "This place is a dump. Why'd you move out of the place on Bagley?"

"I couldn't afford the rent."

"That's 'cause you left pictures. You should of stayed. You could be pulling down five bills a week now, way the business is growing. Hell, you could be a star, rich bitch out in Hollywood, get coke delivered to your door, do maybe one fuck scene per movie and fake that. Jackie Bisset, look at her."

"I'll call the police." Her hand was on the telephone.

He said nothing. Stood there. If she moved.

She said, "If you go now, I'll just forget anything happened. Just leave my keys and the gun. You shouldn't have one. If they find it on you—"

"I get a fine for CCW, maybe ninety days. I ain't on parole, Slick. I'm free as water. See, I was sick, but I'm all better now. Shrinks give me a clean bill of health. You want to see how healthy I am?"

"Roy, I'm going to walk out past you. If you're hungry or thirsty, you can help yourself to whatever's in the refrigerator while I'm gone. But if I find you here when I get back I'll call the police."

He had his knife out now and open, and he was whetting the blade on his woolen sleeve. It made a soft licking noise.

"You call Gramps, tell him what I said? I don't want no interruptions tonight."

She took a step, another. She felt awkward doing it with him watching. It was like the first time she had had to walk across a soundstage with the camera turning. Later the director had told her it was the hardest thing to do in acting. All of her appendages seemed to work independently. She walked and then she was past him and she walked faster and then she was grabbed and spun around and her back hit the door hard enough to buckle the frame. Roy leaned into her, pinning her. He had her right wrist in his left hand, pressed across her left shoulder against the door. He turned the knife this way and that in front of her face so that the blade caught the light.

"Remember *Alley Man*, Slick? The rape in the motel room?"

She struggled. He leaned in harder. Her right shoulder creaked in its socket. He repeated the question. He was breathing just a little harder than normal.

"I wasn't in that one." She paused to catch her own breath.

"You missed something."

"I'll take your word for it."

"Don't worry, though," he said. "We'll make it up to you somehow. Hell, we'll make it better. See, I kept in practice. There was this girl in Ypsi. Retard, you know? But, man, didn't she learn fast."

"I'll kill you."

"That ain't a word you get to use, Slick. Not till you done it." He pushed aside the neck of her blouse with the point of the blade, tracing her collarbone with the blunt edge.

"What are you going to do?"

"Nothing ain't been done to you before. No pay, though, this time. We'll call it a rehearsal."

"Oh, that."

She was relieved, actually relieved.

Chapter Twenty-three

"**Y**ou like oysters?"

Standing at the stove in his apartment, still in his vest and tie and pink shirtsleeves with the white apron on over everything, Gerald Goldstick reminded Donna Macklin of someone. She worked at it.

"No," she said. "I don't like food that springs back."

"That's okay, I'll just scrape them off your steak before I serve it."

She remembered. It was that gourmet cook she used to watch on television in the afternoons, the one who cooked everything in wine and drank off the excess. She had liked him until he got into an accident or something and came out of the hospital Born Again. Everything's got to be recycled these days, she thought, paper and clothing and Christians. Stale.

"You cook steak with oysters?"

"My mother's recipe. They bring out the natural flavor that mushrooms just smother. Also they're good for the libido."

"I thought that was a myth."

"I don't get many complaints."

Conceited little rooster. As if she'd be going to bed with him if there were anything else available in a zipper. Him with his hairless chest and tight little butt in a blue cotton slingshot. Mac had worn white Jockeys as long as she'd known him, dull underwear, and she'd never had any complaints about that part of their relationship. Nor did his little sidepiece, she suspected. Donna had been out of circulation too long. She wondered just when the entire masculine population had gone over to these randy little rodents in colored underwear.

"Open the wine, will you? I'll be through here in a minute."

She said okay and went into the living room where the folding table was set up to do it. Opening the wine, another male job ceded to women. The bottle was cold to the touch. Chilled. Her father, a mid-level connoisseur, had always insisted that any wine that couldn't be served at room temperature wasn't worth serving. So that was another thing that had changed. She bet that when the steaks came they would be lean. Mr. Gerald Goldstick didn't mess around with cholesterol, never mind that the meat tasted like boiled wood. She twisted in the corkscrew and braced the bottle against her stomach and forced down the little levers. The cork came out with a satisfying report. She laid it aside with the screw still attached, leaving a burgundy stain on the white tablecloth, and filled the two glasses. He came out then with the steaks on a tray. She looked at them.

"Jesus, they must have made the cows jog."

"Got to watch the old bloodstream." He used a long-handled fork to transfer the steaks to the china plates.

"I've lost two pounds. You don't have to put me on a diet."

"I'm talking about health. Two more dishes." He spun back into the kitchen, balancing the empty tray on his upraised palm like a waiter.

Actually she had lost just a little over a pound, but her cheap bathroom scales measured in twos, and when the indicator cleared a notch she rounded off the results. She looked slimmest in blue, and she was wearing that color dress tonight, straight up and down without a belt or any other kind of tie or ornament to interrupt the clean line and call attention to her various bulges. With Gerald's encouragement she was reawakening the fashion and practical dressing sense she had had before things got so bad with Mac and Roger that she had stopped caring.

She sipped at her wine. It started out a sip, but as the familiar warmth spread through her system she went ahead and drank off half the glass. Hurriedly she replenished it so Gerald wouldn't notice. She set the bottle back down an instant before he reentered with two dishes balanced on each forearm busboy fashion. He arranged the dishes on the table and took off his apron and held Donna's chair while she sat down.

"What's this green stuff in the cottage cheese?"

"Wintergreen." He sat down opposite her and unfolded his napkin.

"That another of your mother's recipes?"

"Not exactly. Hers called for green onions. But she was married to Dad and didn't have to worry about her breath."

"The soup's cold."

"It's supposed to be. It's gazpacho."

"Gesundheit."

"Funny. Try it."

She took a spoonful, caught herself blowing on it, and swallowed it. After a second she glared at him and grabbed for her wine. This time she emptied the glass.

"Now I know why you chilled it," she gasped.

"Gazpacho takes some getting used to. Eat your steak before it gets cold." He picked up the wine bottle and refilled her glass.

The steak was delicious and she told him so. He executed a little bow sitting down, like a boy at a dancing class. She said, "You were very good in the judge's chambers today."

"I had to be. Flutter seems slow, but he's like a water moccasin if you try to slip something past him. I was impressed with Klegg. You're normally better off hiring a supermarket bag boy to plead a divorce case than a lawyer whose specialty is something else. But he was like a Vegas veteran in there. Your husband isn't so dumb."

"He isn't dumb at all. Some people think he is because he's always so serious. It isn't that he doesn't get the jokes; it's just that he doesn't find them funny."

"He isn't what I expected."

"What were you expecting, a bouncer's build and a broken nose?"

"Something like that. He really isn't very intimidating. He's like a salesman or a junior executive that got stalled."

"I've seen the blood run out of men's faces when they recognized him."

"How many people has he killed?"

"I never asked. I didn't know for sure he'd killed any until recently. I suspected it for years, but I didn't want to bring it up. You know, like when someone close to you is dying. You're afraid if you talk about it, it'll be true. You know it's true, but there's always that little doubt and you hang on to it."

He topped off their glasses. "Didn't he ever talk about it?"

"Never. It's how he got to be thirty-nine, doing what he does. He was doing it when we met. I'm sure of that now, though I didn't want to admit it when we were living together. What kind of wife stays married to a man almost seventeen years without knowing what he does to support them?"

"What tipped you?"

"He was always going off on business trips or working late at the office. Whenever I called the office, his secretary said he was in a meeting and couldn't be disturbed. For a long time I thought he was playing around on me. He was, but that wasn't the reason."

She pushed her plate away and picked up her glass. "I don't know, it just sort of seeped in on me. Sometimes he'd be gone for weeks. Touring his company's branch offices, he said, helping them get organized. Once it was more than a month, and then I got a call saying he was in Detroit Receiving Hospital with a gunshot wound. They said it was an accident. He was hunting in the Irish Hills with a customer who mistook him for a pheasant. He had tubes sticking out all over. I didn't even know he was in the area. He was supposed to be in Chicago. That was in 1972."

"The big gang war," Gerald said.

"I didn't know anything about it. It was only after Mac got out of the hospital that I started paying attention to that kind of thing. Somewhere in there, I don't remember where exactly, I knew. Not *knew* knew, as in having evidence. But as in knowing." She lit a cigarette. She didn't remember getting it out or putting it in her mouth.

"Is that when you started drinking?"

"That came later. I didn't drink at all before then. I didn't like the stuff. Hell, I still don't. But hot fudge sundaes won't get you through the long days and nights alone when your husband's out there killing people."

"I think that's an excuse."

"A damn good one."

"I mean, I think you're dramatizing yourself. It hurt you more to find out your husband was keeping secrets from you. I think if he went on doing what he did and told you about it, you'd still be happily married. Give or take one mistress."

She drank some wine. "You've been hanging around court-appointed psychiatrists too much."

"Maybe."

"I don't think I was happily married anyway. We only got married because I was pregnant. I thought I loved him later, but that was just being used to having him around. Roger's more like him than either of them will admit and that never made it any easier."

"You love your son, though, don't you?"

"Same thing, I got used to having him around. Not even

that, now. I was a rotten mother. Mac wasn't around when Roger needed him to be, and I spoiled him silly."

"Isn't that what mothers do?"

"You better not let the feminists catch you talking like that," she said.

"The feminists aren't here. You are."

"He got mixed up in dope and I was too stupid to see it until it was too late. Or too drunk. He went sour long before that, though. Now he wants—well, forget what he wants. Say I messed up all the way around. I wouldn't have had to if Mac had used the house for something more than just home base."

He was looking at her. "What's Roger want?"

"Forget it, I said. I talk too much. Mac always said I talk too much. I thought it was because he hardly ever talked at all. But since he moved out I haven't been able to stop my mouth from working. How about another slug of wine?"

"You've had enough. He wants to be like his father, right? A killer."

"Let it go, Gerald."

After a moment he sat back. "You know, those things aren't doing your heart any good."

She glanced at the cigarette in her hand, took a puff. "We're all killers. Some of us just like to practice on ourselves."

"No, they're a special breed. You have to be born missing something to go into that kind of work."

"We're all just meat and muscle and bone to someone like Mac." She put out the cigarette, smiled, and laid her hand atop the lawyer's on the table. "I didn't come here to talk about him."

He smiled. "Dessert's in the oven."

"Let it burn."

"What am I, just a sex object?"

"I wouldn't say 'just.' "

God, she was listening to herself.

He sat there a little longer, puffing up. Then he got up and held her chair.

Later, in bed, Goldstick lay next to Donna, looking at the darkened ceiling. He couldn't get over the fact that he was sleeping with a hit man's wife. It was better than oysters.

Chapter Twenty-four

It was past dark when the driver of the last hook-and-ladder turned over its engine, letting it warm up for a minute before gears shifted and the big truck swung around in a wide arc, its headlamps slicing through darkness like a sickle of light. Gravel crunched and it pulled out into the road and changed gears again and throbbed away, no siren.

For what seemed a long time afterward Macklin heard the last man walking around above, something making a chinking noise in rhythm with the footsteps. Handcuffs on a belt. Macklin was sure the man was alone. There was no conversation, and from the sound of things he wasn't making any special effort to be quiet.

The noise stopped. After a second a pebble rattled down the foundation wall, coming to rest on the ground within a foot of where Macklin lay. The man was standing right above him. He willed himself still. If a flashlight came on, a spotlight, he would play dead. If the man came down to investigate . . . He felt the weight of the 10-millimeter pistol lying against his right kidney.

Silence stretched. Then he heard a short zipping noise and then the sound of water running. Something pattered the leaves nearby. An acrid smell came to his nostrils.

Jesus Christ, he thought. I can only go uphill from here.

When it was over the man walked away. For a while Macklin didn't hear anything. Then a car door slammed. It sounded like a gunshot and he jerked involuntarily. A starter ground twice and an engine caught with a roar. Tires turned, zinging a little on flattened grass, then bit into earth. Macklin heard the car stop at the end of the overgrown driveway. The frame rattled a little as it bumped onto the road. He lay listening until the engine noise faded off into the distance. Then he stirred, flexing his muscles one by one, the legs first. He clenched his teeth before trying his stomach muscles, but his ribs held. He was just getting over banging them up the last time. His arms were okay too, a little sore, especially his left, which had folded under when he struck ground, pulling the bicep. He got his hands flat on the earth and pushed himself to his knees, stood. Some miscellaneous scrapes and bruises; he'd be sore later. He'd caught his right jacket sleeve on a thistle or something, leaving a three-cornered rip below the elbow.

He groped around until he found the steps that led up and out of the cellar. They were wooden and going to sawdust and splinters, but he tested his weight on each step, skipping a few when they started to sink. At the top he stopped to take in cool night air tainted with the stench of charred grass and scorched metal. There was no moon. A light hung here and there on the horizon like peaches on a dying tree. He could see his breath in the starlight.

He didn't bother to look at what was left of his car. It would stay there, a blackened shell sitting on wheels with shreds of melted rubber clinging to them, until a wrecking service with a county contract came to tow it away. Instead he walked down to the road, leaving open the gate, its wooden frame hacked to splinters by a fireman's axe. He started on foot in the direction of the main highway.

Something thudded the ground in front of him in the darkness, scattering stones. He unholstered the pistol in a single fluid movement that made him think of a movie cowboy even in the act, thumbed off the safety in the same motion, and fired. Something squealed and was silent. After a moment he stepped forward and lifted the thing by its tail.

Casting the carcass into the brush at the side of the road, he thought: Getting pissed on and killing possums, what next?

Ring, ring.

Standing in the light of an exposed telephone box on a corner three blocks from the house where he was staying, Roger counted the rings. At eleven he pegged the receiver. His dimes clunked down into the pan and he scooped them out. It was just 6:08 by the watch his mother had given him for his sixteenth birthday, which he had just got out of hock. He said what the hell and tried the number again. When no one answered after six rings, he gave up and went home.

The house was dark. The old lady had gone to bed. She always did, just about the time she would have to turn on a light. It pissed him off, because if he turned one on to get upstairs to his room in the attic she would see it under her bedroom door and give him a lecture about sharing the Detroit Edison bill that month. Jesus, it was just a few pennies. Groping his way up the stairs, he bet himself for about the thousandth time that she was one of these old bags who starved to death and then when the cops came to check out the place, they found a quarter of a million socked away in jars and cans all over the house. He'd thought of searching the place but she slept with one eye open for a goddamn light and never went out during the day. He did the shopping for her. She gave him money for it, fives and tens all wadded up in her apron pockets, and he never saw where it came from. Social Security, probably, only she never went out to cash a check. Well, she'd of cashed this month's already. And food stamps, Christ, she should see the looks he got from cashiers and people standing in line, women with their checkbooks out to buy a carton of milk, when he put the stamps on the counter. Like he was picking their pocket. Money wasn't everything, okay, but not having any was sure nothing.

When he was inside his room he closed the door and stuffed a couple of old T-shirts under the crack so he could switch on the light, a string attached to a bare bulb that swung from the ceiling, casting lariats of shadow up the walls until it came to rest. His quarters consisted of a mattress on an iron bedstead and a warped clapboard wardrobe and painted child's bureau with a mirror in need of resilvering. The ceiling came down at a forty-five-degree angle over the bed. He had bumped his head on it twice the first night but he was getting used to it now. The window at one end of the long room was old and discolored and he had to press his forehead against the glass anytime he wanted to see out. He didn't want to, though, after the first time. He had a breathtaking view of the old lady's wash hanging on the line in the backyard and the puddle where she threw out her dishwater because the pipes were always clogging up.

There were two magazines on the bureau, an *American Rifleman* and a *Guns & Ammo* he had bought as soon as he found out there was no TV, but he didn't feel like reading. He looked at himself in the mirror for a little, at his bad complexion, and then he slid the bureau away from the wall and knelt and reached a cloth-wrapped bundle out of an old squirrel-hole he had discovered the first day. He didn't trust the old lady not to search his wardrobe and drawers and probably under the bed while he was out. He unwound the cloth from the .22 semiautomatic and after admiring its racy profile for a moment he stuck it barrel-down into his right hip pocket and faced the mirror with his feet spread and his hands hanging in front of his thighs. Then he scooped out the pistol and drew down on his reflection, snapping on the empty chamber.

"Gotcha, fucker," he said.

No, too gung-ho. Something with more style.

"Too bad, brother."

Yeah, better. He tried it a couple of times, dry-firing the .22 on "brother," until something thumped the floor under his feet. It was the old lady rapping her bedroom ceiling with a broomstick, the one she carried around inside the house for protection in case someone broke in. Roger rewrapped the gun and put it back into its hole, moved the bureau back in front of it, and spent the rest of the evening reading a long article about the new lightweight .45 the army was developing. Then he switched off the light and lay on the bed, mouthing, "Too bad, brother," and grinning at the feel of it in his mouth.

Fucking computer really was down this time.

Randall Burlingame replaced the receiver on the telephone-intercom, not gently, and switched on his desk lamp to glower at the Xerox copy of the West German passport on his desk, at the cherub's face with its high bald forehead and Coke-bottle glasses, an overweight Lionel Atwill, only more amiable-looking. The name underneath was Ingram Wanze, no middle name or initial. Birthplace: Cologne, West Germany. He was as German as a Russian wolfhound.

It was dark outside the window. The cityscape across the river had lost its shape, taking on skeletal configurations made by lighted windows stacked one on top of another, describing cruciforms and inverted pyramids and random letters against many coats of black. On this side, Burlingame's window was the only one showing light on his floor. It was the latest he'd worked in weeks. The passport copy had come through finally from Customs just before quitting time and the computer had shut down just as he was requesting file information on Ingram Wanze. He was missing a double birthday celebration for his daughter and granddaughter, and he was a little afraid to call home again to say he'd be even later than expected. Although Elizabeth, his wife of thirty-three years, never shouted and seldom showed anger in any of the conventional ways, she had a way of saying "I understand" that made him feel as if he had just flashed an orphanage for girls. He was about to call downstairs again when the telephone rang.

"Working, sir," said a young male voice on the other end.

"Okay, let me know as soon as something comes through."

"Er, we lost the input when it went down. Could you repeat the information?"

He ground his teeth on the stem of his cold pipe. "Never mind, I'll feed it through up here."

He went through Louise Gabel's domain, deserted now, her typewriter covered, and down the hall to the office of his assistant. They hardly ever spoke. Ten years Burlingame's senior and awaiting retirement, he had come as part of a package with ten new field agents the bureau director had requested from Washington to expand the local force and replace personnel lost to resignations and transfers. He would come in at noon, stretch out on his sofa, and go home at two if someone remembered to wake him. His secretary had mastered Rubik's Cube and was taking a mail-order course in general accounting.

Without turning on a light Burlingame sat down at the computer console behind his assistant's desk and flipped the toggle, bathing himself in green illumination from the screen. Theoretically the instrument was his, but this was as close to his own office as he would allow one to be installed. Having apprenticed in Records during the Korean war, he had spent too much of his youth memorizing columns of information to surrender his autonomy to a microchip. He entered the code, tolerated the slangy printout greeting some smartass had programmed into the central unit, fed in his request from memory, and sat back to unscrew his pipe and run a straightened paper clip through it during processing. In less than thirty seconds the first line of data came tripping out across the screen, then the next and the next, left to right, faster than a human could type, little green-glowing letters machine-gunning across his vision. He sat there holding the halves of his pipe while the information rolled past, row upon row, stack upon stack, like a roll call of the dead.

Which in truth it was.

The guy that used to be on *Star Trek*, wearing a kinky wig these days and a blue uniform that fit him like the foil on a stick of chewing gum, was under hack for shooting a supposedly unarmed suspect, that old saw, but instead of suspending him or placing him on restricted duty his watch commander had assigned him to the same case. Unreal.

The telephone rang in the dining room. He let his wife get it. Jesus, the *Star Trek* guy had already creamed three parked cars in this one chase. He wanted to watch long enough to see if the guy had any paperwork to fill out after. It would be, let's see, one copy of the report for the file, one for I.A.D., one for each insurance company, that's times three—no, four, there goes a civilian 'Vette caught in the intersection—Christ, he'd qualify for a disability for writer's cramp.

"George, it's that Sergeant Love-something."

He scowled at the screen—shot of the police cruiser's undercarriage shooting up over a steep hill, six hundred dollars' suspension replacement right there, one more copy for the department's insurer—and got up out of the easy chair to accept the receiver from his wife.

"Thought you went home." He leaned against the dining room arch, watching the chase.

"I'm working the double, Christmas coming up," cracked Sergeant Lovelady's voice. "Girl in Traffic just finished running a plate number on a total out in the country, torch job, probable stolen. Her husband's attached to Homicide. She recognized the owner's name and hustled it up here. I thought you'd want to hear it."

Nice close-up of a windshield shattering, cut to a commercial. Pontier turned his back to the screen. "Reel it out."

"Belongs to a two-year-old Mercury Cougar, silver. Registered to Peter Macklin, 10052 Beech Road, Southfield."

"Who called it in?"

"County sheriff's deputy out there name of Connor. That's Charlie Only Needle Needle—"

"Yeah, yeah. You call him?"

"Not yet."

"Well?"

"Okay. Anything else?"

"Then call me."

" 'Kay."

He hung up, shaking his head. When he got back to his chair, the *Star Trek* guy, in civvies now, was having a beer with his partner, who looked like a white Michael Jackson. It was still daylight out. Pontier decided in California each cop got his own secretary to fill out the reports and wondered what he was doing watching this crap while *Mr. Ed* was playing on HBO.

Chapter Twenty-five

"**H**ow was the party?"

"Good, the part I got in on anyhow. Answer these any way that seems right." Burlingame deposited in front of his secretary all but a few of the letters she had had waiting for him.

In fact he had gotten home the night before just in time to kiss his daughter and granddaughter good-bye as they were leaving and help his wife clean up the mess. He had spent half of the rest of the night listening to her tell him she understood.

He went into his office, where he unlocked the top drawer of his desk and read the computer printout sheet once again. He had half hoped he'd dreamed the whole thing, but here it was by morning light, and it was no more believable than it had been at night. It was one of those times when any man over fifty thought of investing in one of those fishing caps with an ornamental beer can on the band and leaving the store to someone who could still get up in the morning without having to brace himself on the night table.

The intercom buzzed. He raised the receiver, his eyes still on the printout.

"Call on one," Mrs. Gabel informed him.

"Who?"

"I'll let him tell you. You wouldn't believe it from me."

He laid down the sheet and punched the button.

● ● ●

The alley behind the yellow brick building stank of rat dung and stagnant water. Macklin tugged on the handle of the scuffed-iron fire door and found it open. The only light in the entryway came from a fifteen-watt bulb that barely managed to illuminate itself. When his pupils adjusted, he pressed a button in the tarnished panel on the wall in front of him. It glimmered and after a long wait the elevator wheezed down like an old man lowering himself into a tub, and the doors trundled open. He went in gun first.

"Fieldhouse."

Air swished. A hammer of pain struck the bone of his wrist and his forearm went numb. The 10-millimeter clattered on the floor. A foot kicked it across the elevator, where the square, graying man in the three-piece suit bent down and scooped it up. Macklin lunged for it and stopped when the bore came up to face him.

"You're slowing down, Macklin," Burlingame said.

Macklin placed his back to the doors, watching the two men who shared the elevator car with him. The one the FBI bureau director had called Fieldhouse was in his twenties, sandy-haired, and good-looking in a male model sort of way. His dark suit and vest fit him well, unlike his superior's, which was starting to show strain at the buttons. Fieldhouse was rubbing the edge of his right hand. Macklin hoped he'd broken it.

He really hated elevators.

Burlingame glanced at the young agent, who pressed the elevator stop button. The car lurched to a halt between floors, and that was the first the killer realized that it had been moving.

"I've heard of these. This is the first one I've seen." The director turned the pistol over in his hands. "I guess you won't tell me where you got it."

Macklin said nothing. Burlingame found the magazine release, popped it out, and worked the slide to eject the cartridge from the chamber. It made a little clattering sound on the floor. Then he returned the empty gun to Macklin, who stood there holding it for a minute, then returned it to its holster. He tugged the waist of his wool jacket down over the butt. Fieldhouse goggled.

"We're all equal here," Burlingame told him, pocketing the magazine. To Macklin: "You called the meeting. I'm not earning your tax dollars hanging around a building we only use for interrogations. What's your business?"

Macklin said, "You picked the spot. I was willing to meet you in your office."

"The lobby of the Federal Building's full of reporters looking for another Daniel Ellsberg. One of them might recognize you on your way up. You know how it works."

"Where's your pipe?"

"Fieldhouse is allergic. I hear you're running your own game now."

The killer grinned wolfishly. "No one ever said that to me before. About running a game."

"Fieldhouse likes that kind of talk. He grew up in front of the tube."

"Fieldhouse counts for a lot."

"He's like a second son to me." Burlingame winked at the young agent. "Put out any good fires lately? Macklin fights them in stairwells," he told Fieldhouse. "He's sort of an urban ranger."

"Fire follows me. I almost got burned again last night."

"That what happened to your coat?"

"We're boring Fieldhouse. What do you know about what's been going on?"

"I know you're running scared or you wouldn't have pulled that bonehead stunt with a pistol against two armed federal agents. What is it about you people don't like?"

"I was hoping you'd tell me."

Burlingame said, "Shit. Macklin, let's get squared around. I don't like killers. I don't even admire them. Last week an eight-year-old kid in Seattle blew off his brother's face playing with a shotgun. I have less things to respect as I get older, and I don't have any at all for a guy who does for money what any eight-year-old kid in Seattle can do without even trying. Aside from all that I don't like you personally. But if I hung out paper on you it wouldn't be just because I don't like you, and I wouldn't send in a psycho with a pregnant Ronson to do it."

"I keep getting that speech. So who would?"

The director was silent.

"Come on, Burlingame. You owe me."

"I owe you shit. The street says Boniface paid you a hundred long ones for the Boblo job. He's getting his hearing like we agreed and we're all back in our places just like we were before."

Macklin reached for one of his slash pockets. Fieldhouse grabbed his arm. The killer relaxed. "Get it out yourself."

Still holding on, the young agent burrowed his other hand into the pocket and came up with a hollow brass cylinder the size of the cap on a ballpoint pen. He patted down the rest of Macklin's pockets and stepped back, handing the cartridge case to his superior. Macklin had gotten rid of the 10-millimeter shells on his way back to the city.

"Who's carrying a Walther these days?" he asked.

Burlingame examined the shell. "MI-6. Scotland Yard. The Sûreté. Any collector with a line on ammunition. It's a popular gun in a lot of places."

"The KGB?"

"Some. The Russians have better weapons, though. Anyway, they're CIA meat."

"Not inside the U.S."

"What do you know, Macklin?"

"I don't *know* anything or I wouldn't be here. But so far I've been jumped by an American ex-Marine, a Chinese jack-in-the-box, and a guy that dresses like the little old winemaker and fires a gun that's most popular with foreign agents. Also, he uses exploding bullets. Not dum-dums, something more sophisticated. Also he rigged my car, which was how he really planned to get me. The shooting was just to make me forget myself; beat the bush, then spring the trap. He's better than either of the others, a professional. I know all the pros in this area and he's not one of them. You throw a wider loop."

"The Russians don't kill for sport, not here," Burlingame said. "You have to bite them on the butt first."

"Before this guy the closest I ever got to Russia was a fifth of Smirnoff's. If he is a Russian."

"You're working, right?"

"I'm a consultant."

"Yeah, and Hitler was chancellor. It's my turn to say come on."

Macklin looked at Fieldhouse.

Burlingame stepped forward and started the car moving. "Fieldhouse, I'm parking you."

"Sir, I'm cleared."

"Not with our friend. It'll just be for a half hour or so. You can go back to the office if you want." The doors opened.

"I'll wait."

When the young agent had stepped out, his superior sent the elevator back up and stalled it in the same location.

"Your friend isn't Russian," he told Macklin. "He's a Bulgarian and his name is Simeon Novo, or at least that's the one he uses in his own country. When he's there, which he isn't often. Most of the time he's out annulling. That's the common accepted contemporary term for killing in the espionage racket. He's either fifty-eight or sixty-two depending on which birth record you go by, and he's in semi-retirement. That means he only kills one or two people a year. I've got a printout as long as my leg back at the office that reads like a primer on international assassination over the past fifteen years, which is when we started keeping tabs on him. The CIA probably has a better one, more thorough."

"How come you have anything on him at all? FBI jurisdiction stops at U.S. borders."

"Washington has a whole bureau assigned to monitor what the CIA is doing. We've got hackers can break into a computer file with a triple security system in less time than you can pick your nose with a nail file. It's like sneaking a peek at your own partner's cards, I know, but what the hell? Last year the Pentagon paid eleven hundred dollars for a staple remover that runs a buck ninety-eight in any stationery store."

"I was right about the KGB, then. It was just a wild guess."

"Well, maybe he's KGB. Our information says he works just as often for the CIA. He's what we call a Dutch door. He swings both ways. His code name on the market is Mantis."

"Jesus."

"Who are *you* working for?" Burlingame demanded.

"Myself."

"We can always sweat Klegg. We know he's involved, and he knows we can scrape up enough on him to keep him in court for ten years, years he doesn't have. He'll blow you rather than let that happen."

Macklin looked around the car and ran his hand behind the rail on both sides.

Burlingame said, "It's not wired. It's the only room in the building that isn't, and it's why we're here. It wouldn't stand up in court anyway."

"I'm working for the daughter of an old friend of Klegg's," Macklin said. "She's got boyfriend trouble. He's threatening to kill her."

"Only she's paying you to kill him first."

"I'm working for her. That's all you get."

"Not good enough. Names."

The killer held up an index finger. "One. Roy Blossom. A local film stud they sprang from Ypsi last month. He was in for carving his initials on a bad driver."

"Where's he live?"

"I don't know. They wouldn't tell me at the hospital, and I didn't feel like putting a gun to their heads."

"We can get that information for you. If you cooperate."

"Right now I just want to know whose list I'm on and why."

"We'll run Blossom through the machine and see what it spits out. Your troubles seem to have started the day you called on Klegg. If there's a connection, we'll find it. But you'll have to let us know what goes on at your end."

Macklin said, "You're sitting on something."

"You're not?"

The killer leaned on the rail.

"Well, I don't shake hands."

"I wouldn't anyway, with you." Burlingame extended the magazine he'd broken out of the other's pistol.

Macklin accepted it.

When the doors opened, Fieldhouse stood out of the way to let Macklin leave the car and fell into step with the bureau director. Outside, the killer turned south while the pair swung north in the direction of the Federal Building. Fieldhouse asked what happened.

"I cut a deal."

"With *him*?" He glanced back over his shoulder at Macklin's retreating form.

"I didn't tell him everything. He doesn't know about Kurof or that we traced Kurof's partner to CIA headquarters. He thinks Mantis is with the KGB. Well, he could be right. The checkers keep changing colors."

"But you told him about Mantis."

"I guess you've got a right to know who's trying to kill you."

"Can we trust him?"

Burlingame walked faster, getting his circulation pumping. The air was damp and cold, more November than October.

"This serviceman was getting set to muster out," he said.

"As the day got closer his correspondence with his wife got steadily more horny. In his last letter he wrote, 'When you meet my plane you better have a mattress strapped to your back.' 'Okay,' she answered, 'but you better be the first man off.'"

They stopped on a corner to wait for the pedestrian signal to change. Fieldhouse was watching the director.

"Macklin's the wife," Burlingame said.

Chapter Twenty-six

The telephone rang while the old man was packing his bags in his room. He let it jangle while he closed the bigger of the two suitcases and spun the combination dial and leaned the straps tight before setting the buckle. He had gotten rid of the Walther and the ammunition and mercury kit and was leaving with no more luggage than he had brought with him. He answered the telephone.

"This is Mr. Brown," said the familiar voice.

"Yes, Mr. Brown."

"It appears that delivery on the package was not accepted."

"Impossible."

"Not according to our man in the Federal Building. The package was seen."

"An error, perhaps."

"An error, yes," said Brown. "But not our man's. Will you rectify?"

"Satisfaction is guaranteed." He pulled his mouth down at his reflection in the mirror atop the bureau. "I will require the same arrangements as before."

"Agreed. We also have more possible contracts for you."

"I am coming."

Breaking the connection, the old man regarded his image sadly. "Simeon, Simeon," he said.

"Miss King, please. Moira King."

"I'll see if she's in," said the woman, and put him on hold.

Waiting, Macklin lay back on the too-soft mattress and stretched his legs under the covers. His arm hurt where he had fallen on it and his calf muscles were stiff from last night's long walk. He had made sure to put several miles between himself and the wreckage of his car before thumbing a ride.

The room was smaller than the others he had rented, a corner bedroom in a hotel converted to apartments except for space let by the day to afternoon lovers and sports fans from out of town. He had showered down the hall and slept two hours, waking by his inner clock to call the telephone offices where Moira worked.

"I'm sorry, Miss King didn't report to work today."

"Is she sick?"

"I'm not permitted to give out information about employees."

He worked the plunger and dialed her apartment. He let the telephone ring twelve times, then hung up. After a moment he kicked aside the covers and sat on the edge of the bed. He was having trouble coming fully awake. In earlier times he would open his eyes to the same thought he had gone to sleep with, his blood glowing like neon gas in his veins. He missed that, and in missing it he acknowledged a thing he had been refusing to recognize for many months. Now it was there, like Red China. He reached for his clothes.

The sky was overcast, that glistening purplish gray that paint always turns when improperly mixed. The cold had sharpened its teeth since his morning meeting with Randall Burlingame. He zipped up his jacket and took his place inside a glassed-in DSR bus stop next to an Errol Flynn gang member in a purple satin jacket and a fat black woman in a cloth coat cracking sunflower seeds between her dentures and spitting out the shells. The Flynn smelled of body odor and pomade. Do it in Detroit, the billboards said.

When the bus came finally he took the backseat, the one

directly over the engine that was hard on the back because of the vibration. Because of that he had it all to himself, the whole width of the bus, with a clear view of the aisle and a short hop to the rear exit. He had been doing these things so long he no longer thought about them, like closing the cover on a book of matches before striking one.

He got off in Redford Township with sharp pains bolting across his lower back, a character in a cartoon shooting stars and little forks of lightning out of the place where it hurt. He shifted the gun to a more comfortable spot. It got better as he walked. His calf muscles ached, but that was all right. They felt tight and ready for anything.

No one was following him, he was sure of that. After parting with Burlingame he had pulled out a couple of tricks to shake any agents the FBI man might have planted on him, and he had long ago discouraged the tail Inspector Pontier had tried to pin on him. It bothered him, though, that he had failed to spot the old man on his back the night before. The others had been easy to nail because they tried so hard to be inconspicuous. The old man *was* inconspicuous. It was the first requirement of the professional "touch"; instinct and reflexes came second and third. You saw old men like him everywhere. Picking him out from the rest was like tracking a drop of fresh water across the Great Salt Lake. Or maybe Macklin was losing his eye along with his energy. In his business it was one of the natural causes.

The security system in Moira King's apartment house was a joke. There was no intercom, just an electronic lock; anyone in any of the apartments could open the front door to a visitor he couldn't see. Macklin studied the row of buttons in the foyer, selected one whose number placed the resident on an upper floor facing away from the door, and pressed it. A moment later a burring buzz sounded. He opened the door and entered.

Moira's was the corner apartment on the second floor. He rapped on the door, waited, rapped again. When no one answered the second time he tried the knob. It turned all the way around and the door opened in. Something spread its dark wings inside his chest.

He brought out the 10-millimeter, stood to the right of the door near the knob, and gave it a push. The waiting gunman smart enough not to fire directly through the doorway would choose to pierce the wall on the side near the hinges.

There were no shots in either location. He fixed his grip on the gun, filled his lungs, and hurtled through the opening, pivoting to flatten out against the wall inside the apartment. He was alone in the living room.

It was messy but in good condition. The sofa was unfolded and the bedclothes were rumpled, tangled. A throw pillow lay on the carpet at its foot. A woman's tailored blue jacket drooped over the arm. The coffee table supported a smeared glass and an ashtray heaped with butts among the dog-eared magazines. Nothing appeared damaged or violently dislodged.

Still holding the gun, he walked over to the kitchenette and stretched to look beyond the four-foot counter that separated it from the living room. The floor was clean.

He thought he smelled something familiar. Then he wasn't sure. Rooms where women slept provided a combination of smells that were always foreign to him. He went into the bathroom. The smell was stronger there, a dank sharp musty odor that was like no other. He knew it now.

Something that looked brown in the sunlight sifting through the silver lace curtains over the window spotted the ivory-colored tiles at his feet. He touched one of the spots with the toe of a shoe. It smeared glutinously.

The curtains were drawn in front of the bathtub, opaque pink plastic with blue fish printed on them. Stepping back, he leveled the pistol along his hipbone and stretched out an arm to slide them apart with a rattling of plastic rings. The movement disturbed a double handful of fat flies, one of which lighted on his cheek next to his nose and had to be brushed away with the barrel of the gun.

His killer's stomach did a slow turn when he looked down and saw why the flies were there.

Chapter Twenty-seven

Feliz Suiza closed the door of the office safe on the morning receipts and went back out into the shop to draw the blinds and turn off all the lights but those in the display window. *My shop*, he always called it, never just "the shop." It was the first thing he had ever owned. A small, very black Cuban with flat features cracked many years beyond his bare forty-two from cutting cane in the hot sun, he had come over on the Freedom Flotilla with his son Tranquillo, who was now a bullpen pitcher with the Detroit Tigers. Tranquillo had used his contract money to finance the shop with the National Bank of Detroit and give it to his father. Feliz had a photograph of his son in his baseball uniform taped to the cash register, and whenever someone came in to pawn a typewriter or redeem a saxophone he would point to it and urge the customer to remember the name Tranquillo Jesus Suiza come playoff time next year.

He was open every day but Holy Sunday and made good money, more than he had ever seen from his laborer's wages, but the habits of a lifetime broke with difficulty and he always took an hour's nap precisely at three. He was on his way to his cot in back when someone banged on the front door. He ignored it and continued walking, but as the banging went on he muttered an oath in Spanish and went back and raised the blind over the door, calling, "We close. Come back later."

The man on the other side of the glass didn't turn away.

He was much older than Feliz, owlish-looking in funny round glasses and a little hat with a yellow feather in the band. A slight pot webbed in a green sweater swelled out through the opening in his topcoat.

"I called you before," the man shouted back, pudgy hands cupped around his mouth. His eyes went from side to side, comic-sinister. "About a gun."

"I said after four."

"It will just take a minute." When Feliz hesitated, the man reached inside the sweater and came up with a handful of bills folded double. The shop proprietor unlocked the door and opened it.

"You said you have a Walther," the man said.

"Come in. Don't shout on the street."

Inside, the man took off his hat. He was bald to the crown. "The gun is new? No previous owner?"

He had a thick, slow accent, not Spanish. He did not look or sound like a police officer, and he was many years older than the detectives who sometimes came to ask Feliz questions. When he did not answer the man's question right away, the man began counting hundred-dollar bills from one hand to the other. The Cuban decided then that he was not a detective. It was too much money to risk on a simple arrest for illegal sale of firearms.

"It is still in the box." He relocked the door and redrew the blind. "Six hundred dollars."

The other pocketed all but six bills but held on to them. "I must see the gun."

Feliz told him to wait. Back in the office he opened the safe and took out the false bottom and removed the box with the gun from among the others. He brought it out and put it on the counter. The man put down an antique candelabra he had been examining, picked up the box, nodded approval at its unscuffed condition, and lifted off the top. He hefted the semiautomatic and checked the empty magazine. "You have ammunition?"

"Yes, but cartridges are extra."

The man took the roll out of his pocket, peeled off four more bills, and laid a thousand dollars on the counter.

"You have been recommended to me as a man to be trusted, a man of silence," he said.

"I see to my business and let others see to theirs." Feliz was looking at the money.

"I need two more men who observe the same philosophy," said the man.

Feliz touched the bills. The man didn't stop him. He tidied them, squaring off the edges. Then he folded them once and tucked them into his shirt pocket, where they bulged like a woman's breast.

"I throw in the cartridges," Feliz said.

Pontier showed the uniformed officer in the hallway his badge and ID and went through the open door into the apartment. There he found Sergeant Lovelady in conversation with a man Pontier recognized from the coroner's office. The sergeant wore a gray waterproof open over his yellow sport coat. Another uniform was standing around plainly wondering what to do with himself and a photographer stood at the window tripping his flashgun at the floor, testing it. They were always doing that. It could make you crazy.

"Somebody's good with a knife," the coroner's man was saying. "I've been a deer hunter twenty years and it's as fine a job of quartering as I've seen. Must've taken him most of the night."

"Night?"

He looked at Pontier for the first time. "Hello, Inspector. Twelve hours anyway, maybe eighteen. Body temperature goes down fast after all the blood's drained away. I'm mostly going by how completely it's congealed. I'll make a more intelligent guess once I get into the stomach downtown."

"We got a name?" Pontier asked Lovelady.

"Moira King's the name on the lease. We got a preliminary

ID from the manager. He's the one called us. Came around to fix the faucet in the bathroom, found the door open, and came in. He said. He didn't want to go snooping in no drawers, run his fingers through her undies, not him. He's downstairs in his office if you want to talk to him. I put a uniform there."

"He our guy?"

"Nah. He threw up in the sink. Guys like him don't even cut up their own meat."

"That bad, huh?"

"Jesus, there's two inches of blood in the bottom of the tub. You'd think he'd of pulled the stopper at least."

"Trouble with these scroats," Pontier said. "No consideration. Anybody see anything?"

"Not yet. Most of the tenants are at work. We'll pump them when they get home."

"What'd this Myra do?"

"Moira. She was something with the telephone company, the manager said. Some pay stubs we found check out. Quiet, no parties, not many visitors. Kind of stuck up, he said. Meaning she didn't fall down and spread her legs every time he said hi."

"Hit it off, didn't you?"

"Guy's a fuck, like every other landlord I ever met. That faucet I told you about? I tried it. Works just fine."

"We got a weapon?"

The sergeant reached into his raincoat pocket and brought out a small square semiautomatic pistol in a glassine bag. "Under the bed. It wasn't there long. Lots of dust bunnies there but the place was clean. It hasn't been fired. There's a little dust in the barrel."

Pontier looked at the coroner's man. "Gunshot wounds?"

"She was stabbed repeatedly. We'll have to wash her off but I don't think she was shot. Guns and blades just don't go together. If you do one you don't generally do the other."

"Nobody we talked to heard shots," Lovelady added.

"Anything else?" The inspector was still looking at the other man, who pulled a face.

"Downtown. Christ, these aren't exactly the ideal conditions to take a smear."

Lovelady said, "There's pecker tracks on the sheets. This ain't your average everyday rape-murder, though. This guy's way off the white line and in the Twilight Zone."

"Where do we stand with the Redford cops on this one?"

"Smack dab in the middle of it. Someone offers to take your enema for you, you don't stake any claims. Question is, do we want this one?"

Pontier stroked his moustache.

"Yeah," he said. "Yeah, I've got a feeling about it. Handle it?"

"I need help I'll call you. You want to see the damage?"

"I'll take your word for it."

On his way out the inspector made room for a pair of uniformed morgue attendants on their way in with a folding stretcher. Lovelady held up a palm, stopping them, and whistled at the photographer. "Hey, Flash Casey, you ready?"

Chapter Twenty-eight

Treat's eye was the color of blue clay at the peephole in his front door. "What's the matter, you use up the last one already?"

"No, I just need heavier artillery," Macklin said. "Open up."

The dealer let him in and set the locks behind him. "What you need? I got a kid in back."

Piano music floated in from another room. Macklin said, "I need a shotgun sawed off short enough to fold a coat over. Twelve-gauge pump. Ithaca, if you've got it."

"I'm all out of Ithacas. I got a Remington but it ain't sawed off. I can do that upstairs."

"If that's all you've got."

"Okay, let's go."

"What about the kid?" Macklin asked.

"He can use the practice."

The music sounded pretty good to the killer, but he followed Treat into the back bedroom and up the tight staircase to the attic workshop. There the little dealer broke a new Remington shotgun with a square hickory slide out of the wall rack and used an oily rag to wipe off the cosmoline and removed the barrel. After wrapping a cloth around the barrel to protect the steel, he clamped it into the vise on the bench and looked at his visitor.

"Be four hundred."

"It's a lousy hundred-buck fowling piece," Macklin protested. "Not even worth that, with that clumsy damn slide."

"Hey, I'm at considerable risk here. Guy with my record, I'm looking at a year's tour of beautiful downtown Jackson State just for cutting down this barrel."

They agreed on three hundred finally. Macklin took the bills out of his emergency stash and Treat put them away in a drawer of the workbench. Then he scored the outside of the shotgun barrel with a pipe die, selected a hacksaw with a shiny titanium blade from a row of them over the bench, and began cutting. The rasping was like labored breathing in the closeness of the room.

When the thirteen-inch section he had measured off came free, he laid it aside, used an emery cloth on the end of the remainder to smooth the harsh edge, and unwound the vise. The barrel was now no longer than a man's forearm.

"Stock too?"

Macklin nodded, and Treat used a screwdriver to remove the three screws that held the hickory stock in place, then clamped it into the vise and cut off the shoulderpiece with a fine-toothed finishing saw, leaving only the pistol grip. It was the work of a few minutes to reassemble the shotgun. From grip to muzzle it measured less than two feet. "This short she's just as hairy from both ends," Treat warned, handing it over.

"Not if you know how to handle it." The killer reached into an open box of twelve-gauge shotgun shells on top of a stack and took one out to examine it. "Double-ought?"

"Uh-huh. Steel, though. Not lead."

The killer made a face but fed the shell through the bottom loading gate and worked the slide, racking it into the chamber. Elevating the weapon, he watched with approval as the slide glided back down into place without help. "You've done some work on it."

"I wouldn't of had to, it was an Ithaca," Treat said. "Prewar, anyway, not that shit they crank out now. You going to carry it around with one up the pipe like that?"

"What good's a watchdog with his teeth in his pocket?"

"Blow off your foot."

"My foot." Macklin fisted out a handful of shells, filled the magazine, and put the rest in a pocket of his coat. Then he took off the coat.

Treat said, "What you doing? I got to get back to the kid."

"I thought you said he needed the practice."

"Well, you know, I get paid to give him lessons, he tells his mother I wasn't there most of the time, my business falls off. Maybe they wonder what I'm doing when I ain't there."

"You trying to get rid of me?"

"Well, in a nice way." He tried a grin.

Macklin finished folding the coat over his arm with the shotgun under it and jerked his head toward the stairs. Treat hesitated, looked at the gun, then got up and started that way. Sideways, keeping an eye on the man behind him.

"What's got you jumping?" Macklin demanded.

"Nothing. I just hope you don't trip on a step with me in front of you."

"I'd be sorry as all hell."

"Just don't forget about that stuff I left with a friend," Treat said. "I mean, accident, heart attack, a tree falls on me when I'm cutting the grass, it don't make no difference, stuff goes to the cops."

"Don't flex at me, Treat. I'll cut you off at the roots."

They descended the steep staircase, Macklin holding the bundled weapon vertically. The piano was still playing.

"Kid's good," Macklin said.

"He's got a good teacher."

It sounded too jaunty for the dour little gun runner. Macklin hung back a step while the other preceded him out of the bedroom. He saw movement then, a dark leather jacket glistening in the hallway, a flash of faded denim on the other side. He swung the shotgun level and pulled the trigger. The room swelled. Fire leapt, and Treat's back and the two men in jackets dissolved in smoke.

The silence after the roar rang. For an instant Macklin held his ground. Fibers from the blasted coat floated around in the air. Then he bounded forward, almost tripping over the gun dealer's body in the doorway. Treat lay in a spreading puddle of red, his shirt in bloody tatters on his back and smoldering, on top of a black man in a Levi's jacket with all of the middle of him gone. A .32 revolver lay on the floor nearby.

The floor bounced and Macklin swung right, shotgun foremost, toward the end of the hall leading to the exit. The black leather jacket stopped running then and whirled, light glinting off shiny nickel in his hand.

"Stop!" Macklin worked the slide with a loud double clack.

Instantly the black leather jacket dropped his gun and threw up his hands. "Don't, mister! I'm cool!"

He was barely half Macklin's age, white, tall, and reedy, with shoulder-length blond hair that looked greasy in the light. His skin was the slick gray of chewed paper. He was shaking.

The killer stepped over the bodies, lowering the weapon slightly. In another room the piano went on tinkling, and Macklin knew then that he was listening to a recording.

"Forget your name," he said. "Who bought you?"

"Bought me?"

"One." Macklin shouldered the Remington.

"Mister—"

"Two." He braced himself.

"I didn't—"

"Three."

"No!" It was a shout. "I don't know his name, mister. A little old guy with glasses and a funny hat. He split a hunnert between Rolly there and me down at the arcade and said they was another two hunnert in it for us when we offed a guy."

"I'm the guy?"

"You look like what he said. It was just the money, mister. I got a yard-and-a-half-a-day itch, I can't ask no questions. He said you'd be coming here soon."

"Treat in it?"

"Treat—you mean the little guy? Not at first. The old guy, he talked to him, brought him around, kind of. Mister, you let me go, I'd just as soon not—"

"Go."

"What?"

Macklin lowered the gun and let the short barrel droop. "Get out."

The young man hesitated, then started backing down the hall, his hands still in the air. When he reached the living room arch, he turned around and ran stumbling to the front door and tore it open. It drifted shut behind him but not before Macklin heard the shots, two loud nasty shredded pops very close together. Then silence.

Someone groaned.

Macklin turned and looked down at Treat. The fingers of the dealer's one visible hand plucked at the floor. He was lying on his face on top of the dead black man, Rollo, saying something that was muffled by the corpse's denim jacket.

"Fuckstlsht."

The killer bent down, grasped a handful of Treat's brush-cut hair, and lifted his face free.

"Fucking steel shot." The words were slurred through spittle and blood.

"Treat."

"Lead've done the job quick."

"Treat, who's got the information on the guns you've sold?"

"I don't sell guns. I give music lessons."

"It's Macklin, Treat. Who'd you leave the stuff with?"

"Macklin?"

"Yeah. The stuff."

"Ain't no stuff."

"Too late for that," Macklin said.

"Ain't no stuff, that's the joke." He spasmed, drooling blood, and the killer realized he was laughing. "I'm going to write that shit down, hear it read back to me in court?"

Macklin let go of his hair. Christ, there were pellets caught in it. "Fucking steel shot," he said.

"Fuckstlsht." Treat was twitching all over now, the end close.

Decoys. Rolly and his partner, dead by now on the front lawn. Flush the game and catch it when it breaks. Macklin was supposed to have been the one coming out the door. A siren wound up far away, high wail switching to yelp at corners and intersections. Mantis, whatsizname, Novo, would have to abandon the trap soon. But not before the police came and sealed off the house.

Acting out of habit, Macklin retraced his steps over the bodies and picked up the ejected shotgun shell, pocketing it. He fingered a fresh one out of the coat over his arm—evil-smelling, a charred hole in the wool big enough to put his head through—and poked the shell into the magazine. Then he climbed the stairs.

From up there he could hear more sirens joining the first. He found the three hundred dollars he had given Treat in the workbench drawer and put it in his wallet. He looked around at the boxes and cases of ammunition stacked on the floor, the guns on the walls. A man could hold out there for a week if they didn't set fire to the house.

Alone in the cramped room, Macklin grinned.

He went through more drawers until he found a carton of Pall Malls and a book of matches. Leaving the cigarettes, he took the matches, tugged a wooden case full of red-and-white cans marked SMOKELESS POWDER out of the knee hole in the bench, tore a handful of ballistics charts off the sloped ceiling, and stuffed the paper into the spaces between the cans. Then he set fire to the paper and hurried toward the stairs, the shotgun tucked under his arm.

The end of the hall opposite the living room opened into a small kitchen with a breakfast nook and a refrigerator and electric stove and a sink stacked high with dirty dishes. The back door was dead-bolted and required a key to unlock it from either side. The key wasn't in the lock. He stepped back, clamped the shotgun to his hip, and blasted the lock and four inches of heavy wooden door around it into the backyard.

The sirens were in front now, growling down. Car doors slammed in ragged succession like a string of firecrackers going off. A woman's bored voice throbbed out of a police radio turned up to full volume, the words distorted and crackling with static. Macklin retrieved the spent shell and waited.

The first explosion shook the walls. In the ringing echo following the thud he heard voices shouting. He refolded his coat over the shotgun, the gaping hole inside, opened the splintered door, and went out.

The tiny backyard was enclosed by a six-foot board fence. Macklin started around the side of the house just as the second blast ripped off the roof and burst every window in the building. A cloud of flying glass just missed him. He ran through a shower of debris, slammed into a uniformed police officer back-pedaling to get clear of the falling wreckage, spinning him around, and found himself face-to-face with a big black police sergeant washed in the orange light of the flames.

He froze. The shotgun bundled in the coat was pointed at the blue-covered belly bulging over the man's gun belt.

"Get the hell out of the way!" bawled the sergeant, seizing Macklin's arm and shoving him toward the sidewalk. "Can't you damn gawkers see the whole place is going up?"

A large crowd had begun to gather on the sidewalk. They were watching the flames rolling out of the windows on the top floor and shouting encouragement and obscenities at a pair of officers trying in spite of the searing heat to get to the thin, long-haired body lying in front. Seeking the open, Macklin made his way through the press of bodies and official cars parked all over the street. Behind him, cases of small-arms ammunition were going up in cracks and pops.

Chapter Twenty-nine

"**Y**es?"

"Klegg?"

"Yes."

"Macklin. Any calls?"

"You son of a bitch."

Macklin, standing with his back to the wall in the hallway of the administration building at Wayne State University, scowled absently at a pair of students walking by hand in hand. They were both men. He changed hands on the telephone receiver.

"Cops found Moira already?"

"Pontier was just here. He's got a bulletin out for you. You're wanted for her murder."

"You know it wasn't me."

"It might as well have been. She hired you to protect her from that animal."

"She hired me to take care of him."

"You didn't do a very good job."

"How'd the police find out I was involved?"

"Who cares? She was as close to a daughter as I ever came, and now she's dead."

"I told Burlingame at the FBI I was looking for Blossom. His computer must have turned up Moira. He must have something going with the cops."

"He called too. He wants you to call him. He left a number."

"I've got his number."

"This one's different, he said." Klegg read it off. Macklin committed it to memory.

The lawyer said, "Listen, you better give yourself up. The police have weird ideas about men who murder women and then mutilate their bodies. They'll shoot first and claim resisting arrest later."

"It's not my skin you're worried about. You're afraid of being charged as an accessory."

"You son of a bitch. I was going to help her make something of her life. I was going to pay her way through law school."

"She was going to let you?"

"I didn't get the chance to tell her."

"It galled her to have to ask you to help save her life," Macklin said. "Can it be you really don't know what she would've told you to do with your offer?"

"Get yourself another divorce lawyer." The line clicked and buzzed.

Macklin pressed down the fork, then fed another quarter into the slot and dialed the number Klegg had given him. Burlingame's voice came on after the first ring.

"Killers' hotline. Free-lance touches and ex-Mafia hit men a specialty."

Macklin paused. "How'd you know it was me?"

"I've never given the number out before. It's a new addition to the office system, supposedly tap-proof. It doesn't go through the switchboard and puts out some kind of signal that squelches listening devices. I figure it's good for about two weeks, until the electronics industry finds a way around it. Kind of dropped the ball there with the King woman, didn't you?"

"Go to hell."

This time Burlingame hesitated. "I didn't know it was personal."

"What'd you turn on Blossom?"

"Uh-uh. You first."

Macklin leaned his shoulders back against the wall. Classes were starting and the hallway traffic had slowed to a trickle.

"Your spy in Homicide'll be reporting an explosion in a house in Taylor any time now," he said. "Two men dead inside, the owner and a black man named Rolly. The owner's name was Treat. He's in your files if you're up on your Detroit area gun runners. Another dead one in the front yard, name unknown. Cops should have a sheet on him and Rolly. The two inside were shotgunned. It's my guess the coroner's men will dig two seven-sixty-fives out of the stiff out front. Unless they exploded."

"Our friend?"

"His style. Man's got moves."

"Like him, huh?"

"I'll send his widow a card, that's what you mean."

"Bullshit. You're having more fun than you've had in years. He wasn't the one scattershot the two inside, though."

"No, he wasn't."

"Uh-huh." The FBI man stopped talking again. Macklin thought he heard a match striking. "What makes you think we've got someone in Homicide?" The words broken up while he puffed the tobacco into life.

"*Your* style. Now you go."

"We got an address on Blossom from Ypsilanti." He recited a number and street in Melvindale. "He's working in the salt mines under the river there, the day shift. We're waiting on a court order to go in and get a look at the hospital records on his stay there. I've got a hunch but I don't want to say anything about it until I know. Macklin?"

"I'm here."

"I wasn't sure. You were awful quiet. I guess you liked her."

"What else you got?"

"It for now. We aren't making any moves on Blossom before we see the stuff from the hospital. What about you?"

"Have Pontier lift the APB on me, can you?"

"I don't think I can get him to do that. Also, we're talking accessory on those two in Taylor. Another count should anything happen to Blossom."

Macklin laughed dryly. "You got a lot to talk about, after Viola Liuzzo."

"Jury found for us in that one. Anyway, that was Hoover."

"You guys blame everything on Hoover. Like you were all wired into him and he was working the buttons."

"I'll talk to Pontier. It won't do any good."

"Call you later."

"Watch what you say if it's after working hours. I can get calls forwarded to my house from this line, but it won't be eavesdrop-proof that last six miles."

"I'll talk in a high voice and use an accent."

Burlingame chuckled. "Hey, that was pretty good. You're coming along fine."

"Deputy chief on two, Inspector."

Pontier, in his shirtsleeves with the cuffs turned back once, took a sip of the coffee Sergeant Lovelady had brought him and lifted the receiver, punching the button. "Afternoon, sir."

"You've been on this flamethrower thing a week now," said the voice with the music behind it, "Cabaret" this time. "I assume you're about to make an arrest."

"As a matter of fact we are, sir, but for a different murder in Redford Township. Same man. I don't expect to hold him, though, not on that charge."

"Why on earth not?"

"Because he didn't do that one. We know who did but we aren't picking him up just yet. What he is, we're using him as bait. Things break right we can bust the whole thing wide open when they get together."

"I've been meaning to talk to you about your vision of official procedure, Inspector. I don't think you could draw a straight line between two points if you had a ruler."

Jesus, now it was "Rocky Mountain High." Pontier hated John Denver. "Sir, I think we can wipe the board clean on two murders in Redford on top of the flamethrower thing and take a contract killer and a psycho off the street with this one bust."

"You promised me a tie-in to organized crime."

"Well, we're still thumping on that." Go ahead, tell him about the Russians and the FBI, we're in James Bond country now. Remember the road? Backache all the time because they haven't designed a car seat yet that can be sat on eight hours at a stretch, call in Code Three and get one mouthful of tuna fish on white when some scroat with a sawed-off takes the head off a liquor dealer right around the corner. "Very least we got a guy used to do heavyweight work for the wise guys. Press'll treat it the same."

"Oh, you know how the press thinks? There's an opening in Public Information if you're interested."

"Sir, there's always an opening in Public Information. I'm just saying we're on the hot box now and it's going to blow anyway, so we might as well be on top of it when it does. Be there to catch the pieces, if that's not too much to try to get out of a metaphor."

Denver was still singing. The song went on and on, like the flu. "Okay. You know who to call when it goes down."

Yeah, and if that's at two in the morning? Aloud he said, "You'll be the first."

Lovelady was still in the office when he hung up. The fat sergeant stirred himself from Pontier's Academy class picture on the wall to lay a scribbled message on his superior's desk.

"From the Taylor Police," he said. "That four-alarmer today?"

Pontier squinted at Lovelady's scrawl. "Three dead gunshot."

"Two with a shotgun. Maybe more; the upstairs is gone. No IDs yet but the house was in the name of a guy named Treat. Maybe you remember it."

"Treat."

"Fire cops said the place had to of been full of dynamite or powder, way it went up. Coming clear?"

"Gun runner. We had him down here a couple of times on gang shoots, nothing stuck. If it's him."

"I pulled his file. Address checks out. Do we want it?"

"No. Christ, no. They're starting to call me the garbageman already in the burgs. Just leave your unsolved murders out at the curb for Pontier to pick up. But set up a liaison, offer them the use of our facilities in return for a pipeline. Murder rate's gone up a half a percent since someone pricked Macklin's hide."

"You got Macklin on the brain, maybe."

"Maybe. But he has to get his hardware from someplace, and Treat was first-string. Just for now I'm going to look on every K that crosses this desk like it had Macklin's thumbprint on it and blow out the chaff later."

"I put men on Blossom's place like you said. Melvindale cops said okay as long as we don't shoot any innocent civilians. Then they don't know anything about it."

"That's as good as carte blanche. You can fire a cannon in any direction these days and not hit an innocent civilian."

"I saw a T-shirt—" Lovelady said, and stopped.

"What?"

"I saw a guy wearing this T-shirt in the supermarket the other day. Just something I thought of. It said, 'Kill 'em all and let God sort 'em out.'"

"I like it." Pontier played with a pencil. "We'll see it gets put on Macklin's headstone."

Chapter Thirty

Macklin returned to his motel room, a fairly large one maintained by a nationwide chain, with a television set and its own bath and a telephone he didn't trust because using it meant going through the switchboard in the lobby. He tossed his paper-bag-wrapped package onto the bed and peeled out of his sport coat. It was cheap polyester, bought to replace the blasted hunting jacket he had discarded and the good checked sport coat that had blown up with his car, and it was uncomfortably hot, but it covered his pistol and didn't attract as much attention as walking around in shirt-sleeves in the brisk weather.

He experienced a moment of panic when he got down on one knee to feel under the bed and couldn't find the sawed-off Remington, but then his fingers closed around the barrel and he pulled it toward him carefully. A friend of his father's had died with a double load of buckshot in his belly after climbing over a barbed-wire fence and then pulling his shotgun barrel-first between the strands, where the triggers caught. At least, that was the story his father had told him at the funeral. Whatever its truth, the story had made an impression on the boy.

He unloaded the gun on the bed and slid the cheap cleaning kit he had purchased with the sport coat out of its bag. He took his time polishing the inside of the barrel and wiping excess oil off the action. After reloading he put the gun back under the bed and unholstered the 10-millimeter to check the load. In this manner he managed to kill twenty minutes.

His stomach growled, a long low intestinal complaint that was familiar to him. He hadn't had anything to eat all day except a corned beef sandwich on stale rye with a glass of milk at a diner, and if he decided to eat anything more it would just be something light to quiet his stomach. His blood pumped faster and purer on an empty belly, feeding his brain and sharpening his instincts and senses. Predators in the wild hunted only when they were hungry. He had survived to this age following their example. To change would be worse than to invite bad luck.

His watch read ten after four. He called time to confirm it and switched on the television set. He knew he needed sleep but he was wide-awake. At length he made himself comfortable on the bed to watch an *Ironside* rerun on channel 2. Something about a crazed gunman out to kill the policewoman assigned to Chief Ironside's detail. At the climax he wasted time telling the woman what was going to happen to her and how clever he was, giving the Chief and his assistants time to get there and kill the gunman and rescue the woman.

Happened every time, on television. Killer had to have good lines.

When the show was over he turned it off and stretched out and even napped a little. He woke precisely at six without having dreamt, splashed some water on his face in the bathroom, and got out the shotgun again. It was the work of a few minutes to fashion a makeshift shoulder sling out of his belt. When he put on the sport coat, the hem came down just low enough to conceal the barrel. Standing in the middle of the room, he practiced swinging it out a couple of times, then fixed the holstered pistol into the inside pocket of the coat and went out. It was almost completely dark outside. The days were getting shorter faster.

• • •

A stout, gray-haired man in a charcoal suit was using Roger's favorite public telephone when he got there a few minutes past six. The man's briefcase stood on the sidewalk near his leg with a beige trench coat folded over it. Roger saw guys like him all the time, always on the telephone, and not one in ten ever wore the damn coat. He wondered if the sleeves were even real.

Talking to his wife from the sound of it. Guys that had been married a long time never called their wives by their names, or by anything else. Not even "dear" or "honey." They just talked, and it was like they knew each other so well they could tell it was them being talked to without having to ask. Roger hoped no one would ever know him that well.

He cleared his throat and shifted his weight from one foot to the other, making it obvious he was waiting. He thought of saying something to the guy, maybe even reaching out and breaking the connection himself, and a week earlier he would've, but his nerves were better now. Finally at 6:07 by the bank clock across the street the guy pegged the receiver and picked up his briefcase and folded the trench coat over his arm and smiled tight-lipped at Roger and walked off. Roger jumped on the instrument and dialed the number he had memorized.

The telephone rang seven times. He was starting to lean against the box, resigned now, waiting for ten so he could hang up and go somewhere for a drink, when the line clicked and a voice Roger had never heard before said hello.

The address Burlingame had given Macklin belonged to the back half of a duplex on Dix Road in the downriver community of Melvindale, an old frame building with split and curling shingles on the roof and the white paint rubbed down to leaden gray in spots. The lawn was shaggy and sprouting weeds in the dirty moonlight.

It was an eight-block walk from the bus stop. Although there had been seats available aboard the DSR, Macklin had stood throughout the ride because the shotgun under his coat would not let him sit. The only other passenger not seated was an old black man in a cloth cap, whose pained expression whenever the bus clattered over broken pavement or took a corner too fast advertised a bad case of piles. From time to time he and Macklin exchanged sympathetic glances.

Had Macklin more of a sense of humor, he might have reflected with amusement upon the irony of busing killers out of the city into the suburbs.

"Hey."

Stretched out on the musty-smelling mattress in the guest room on the second story of the house across the street, Detective First Grade Arthur Connely came out of a light doze and rolled over to look at his partner seated on a rickety wooden chair at the window. Officer Richard Petersen, Uniform Division, on temporary assignment with C.I.D. Homicide, was little more than a dark bulk against the slightly lighter outline of the glass. "What you got?" whispered Connely.

"Male cauc, five-ten and a hundred and eighty." A twisting sound in the darkness, Petersen adjusting the infrared binoculars. "Around forty."

"Going in?"

"Heading that way."

"That's our guy."

The uniform, in plainclothes tonight, pressed the speaker button on his headset. "Baker two, look alive."

"Shut the fuck up," crackled a voice over the earphones. "I want orders from a guy in a blue bag I'll join the park patrol."

"What's he doing now?" Connely asked.

"Walking. Looking around a little. He's at the driveway. . . . Shit."

"What?"

"He's walking past."

"Keep tracking him. Pontier says this guy's a pro."

Dix Road declined steeply toward Outer Drive, where traffic was swishing by heavily between shifts at the Ford Rouge plant. After passing the duplex Macklin walked all the way down to the corner, then crossed the street and started back up the shadowed side. Darkness was no obstacle to the infrared equipment he knew was trained on the house, but the trees and parked cars on that side would help break up the continuity of any attempts to track his movement.

A big blue 1969 Mercury was parked just below the crest of the hill. The front door on the passenger side was unlocked. He opened it and reached in and flipped the automatic transmission out of gear, then stepped back out of the way. For a long moment the car didn't move, and he was thinking of giving it a push when the pavement creaked under a tire and the vehicle began rolling backward down the slope. It picked up speed as it rolled, and he turned his back to it and resumed walking.

"What?" Connely was sitting on the edge of the mattress now, wide-awake.

"I'm not sure." Petersen adjusted the glasses. "I saw something moving. There! Guy walking."

"Him?"

"Can't tell. Damn the trees."

The detective got up. "Let's have a look."

Petersen was pulling the strap off over his head when a horn blared not far away. Brakes screeched and a tremendous walloping wham splintered the air.

"Jesus Christ!" Connely fumbled for his sheep-lined jacket.

"Baker two, Baker two."

"Fuck that. Let's go!"

The uniform tore off the headset and hurried off after his partner.

Standing in the doorway of a house two lots down from the duplex, Macklin watched the two men running down the street in the direction of Outer Drive, where other horns were blasting now, the traffic knotted around the collision site. He had already seen two others break cover from the bushes next door and hurry that way. He waited two beats, then stepped out and continued his path up the street.

The house described an *L*, with Blossom's number etched in rusting wrought-iron script over the door in the short rear section at the end of the driveway. The only window visible in that section was lighted. Macklin tried the door, then used the edge of his driver's license to slip the antique latch and mounted a steep rubber-paved staircase lit by a dim bulb in an amber globe over the landing. At the top he paused, listening for footsteps on the other side of the flat wooden door in front of him. There were none, but he heard voices inside. He couldn't make out the words.

He thought about that, then decided that anyone talking with Blossom in his home was an enemy. This door he didn't try. Swinging out the shotgun, he braced himself, threw a heel at the lock with all his weight behind it, and let his momentum carry him forward as the door flew open and slammed against the wall inside. He glimpsed movement in front of him, a flash of light-colored shirt in a dark coat, and released a charge. A full-length mirror mounted on the wall opposite the door collapsed, showering tiny reflections of himself all over the floor.

Without pausing to assimilate, he swung right in the direction of the continuing voices, but this time he curbed his impulse to fire. On the bluish TV screen in front of him two scantily dressed women were beating up a gangling young dark-haired man under the rustling racket of a mechanical laugh track.

Macklin was alone in the apartment with a rerun of *Three's Company*.

From the sidewalk across from the duplex, the explosion inside was a massive hollow *crump*, simultaneous with a throb of brighter light at the window, and Roy Blossom's first surprised thought was that the television set had blown up. But then logic came rushing in to fill the vacuum and he recognized it as the report of a shotgun contained in a small room.

He had gone to a restaurant on Oakwood for supper and had been on his way back home when a loud crash from the direction of Outer Drive told him another damn fool had tried to nose his way into the rush-hour traffic at the loss of his fenders. As he came within sight of the duplex two men had come running out the front door of the house across the street and gone down that way. Gawkers, although they both looked too young to be visiting the elderly couple who lived in the house. Blossom wondered if they were relatives. Then he had spotted a third man turning into his driveway, and as the man passed beneath his own lighted window, he recognized him as the one he had seen going into and coming out of Moira's apartment house a couple of nights before. The man's posture as he walked was unnaturally stiff, as if his back hurt. Well, that was what came of balling girls half his age. Blossom had waited on the street, absently opening and closing the clasp knife he had taken from his pocket.

Now, as lights in private houses on both sides of the street sprang on in the echo of the blast, he turned around and hurried back the way he had come. By the time he reached the restaurant where he had just eaten he was out of breath and had to wait, gasping, his pulse hammering in his ears, before he was steady enough to lift the receiver off the pay telephone on the wall in front of the cash register and fumble two dimes into the slot. He listened to the purring, saying, *"Come on, come on,"* and then a voice greeted him with the number he had just dialed.

"This is Blossom," he barked, breaking in before the voice had finished. "Let me talk to Mr. Brown."

Chapter Thirty-one

He didn't invest any more time watching great comedy on the black-and-white set. It was an episode he had seen anyway. Instead he allowed the shotgun to subside back under his sport coat and let himself out the door.

The fire exit at the rear of the lobby was chained and padlocked. Macklin considered blasting through it, then decided not to risk a faceload of ricocheting pellets from the steel door and went back out the way he had come in, swinging out the Remington as he opened the door. He looked into a red Irish face as big and close as a curious gorilla's at the zoo.

"Freeze, motherfucker!" A nickel-plated magnum came up in two outstretched hands.

Macklin's finger was tightening on the shotgun's trigger when hurrying footsteps rattled to his left. The Irish cop, still gasping from a hard run, twitched his face in that direction. Realization of the mistake came in an instant, and he was correcting himself when Macklin swung the Remington's butt. It collided hard with the other's hands and the magnum flew glittering off the front stoop into the dewy grass. The cop grimaced, opening his mouth to curse, and the barrel came back the other way and gonged along the side of his jaw. As he reeled backward Macklin fired over the head of the young man running up on him with something dark and gleaming in his hand. The muzzle flare washed them all in light for a pulsing microsecond, catching the young man in mid-dive for the ground, his partner falling off the stoop, Macklin throwing himself the other way. His momentum carried him down to one knee and jarred loose the belt sling. He lurched upright and forward without pausing while the shotgun slid down his leg and fell to the ground. Running, he left it there. From that point on it was excess weight anyway.

"Stop! Police!"

A swallowed *blam* rent the air left intact by the shotgun blast. Macklin thought he heard the bullet shrilling over his head, but he put it down to imagination. You seldom heard them coming from a magnum. In any case he didn't stop. The night welcomed him as one of its own.

"Radio call, Inspector!"

Lovelady had thrown open the door to Pontier's office without knocking. The fat sergeant was out of breath, although he couldn't have run more than twenty feet from the monitor in the squad room. Pontier, on the telephone, knew the answer to his question before he asked it.

"Who?"

"Connely and Petersen."

He slammed down the receiver without saying good-bye—forgetting even in the act to whom he'd been talking—and hastened out of the office behind the sergeant. He heard the telephone begin ringing as he left. He kept going.

Burlingame, working late, counted sixteen rings before giving up. Less than a minute had passed since his last attempt to get through to Pontier, which had ended, as had all the previous ones, in a busy signal. The man spent as much time on the horn as every other police inspector the FBI man had ever known.

In between tries he had called other sources in an effort to lift the APB on Macklin, but all had declined, maintaining that only the officer in charge of the investigation had that

authority. Which was pure bullshit, but go identify yourself
as federal and try to tell a city man what to do. Now the
officer in charge was either out or not answering his telephone. Burlingame, himself a Bell fetishist, knew that men of
their persuasion would sooner pull out before sexual climax
than sit by placidly and let a telephone go on jangling.

Cradling the receiver, he told the formal portrait of the
President of the United States hanging on the wall opposite
his desk that something was happening.

"Honey? More coffee." Blossom held up his empty cup.

The waitress, a lumpy blond girl in her late teens with
dark circles around her eyes, filled it from the carafe, glancing at him curiously. He ignored the look and she walked
off. She didn't have much up top, but he admired the way
her buttocks moved under the white uniform, like—what's
that line?—like two cats fighting under a blanket. Any other
night he might have been working on her. But he was
waiting for Brown to call him back and he didn't want
anything to distract him from the telephone. Christ, if someone tried to answer it before he did, he'd use the knife on the
bastard.

He was hyper, really wired. He should've made his call
from farther away, some other place where the help
wouldn't wonder what he was doing back after eating there
just half an hour before. Where he didn't have to keep
looking at the door and seeing the old guy coming in with
the shotgun, Jesus, seeing him just like he was there, that
face with its down-drawn lines and a splattergun short
enough to hide under his cheap sport coat, cut back beyond
the choke so that the pattern spread a yard for every foot,
clear the whole restaurant like a firehose. Blossom could see
it happening.

His imagination had always been extra vivid. Once when
he was in junior high he had had the same nightmare three
nights running, about putting his hand through a hole in a

wall and having dozens of rats come squirming up his arm, squealing and slashing at him with their sharp little fangs, and after that he had stayed awake for a week before exhaustion took him. Then he had it again. He had slept in some dumps with holes in the walls since then and every time he looked at one of the holes he still saw the rats clear as anything. He didn't even have to think about them and there they were, all slick gray like seals, fangs showing outside their lips. The last time he had seen them, four male attendants were required to strap him to his bed in Ypsilanti. The time before that had been just before he cut up the colored guy in the parking lot.

Now he was afraid to look around him too closely. The restaurant was in an old building and there might be a hole in one of the walls.

The telephone rang and he slopped coffee on himself putting down the cup. His waitress was just passing the instrument. He beat her there by half a step.

"Mr. Blossom?"

He recognized the familiar burring voice and said, "Where the hell you been? Didn't Green tell you my ass is out?"

"Obviously not too far, or you wouldn't have been sitting there poisoning your system with caffeine for the past ten minutes."

How in hell did he know that? "It's my ass, I guess I know when it's out. Who's the guy with the sawed-off, he one of yours? 'Cause if this is a cross I'll carve on you so good, your friends'll give up looking for the pieces."

"Very colorful. But we gain nothing by threatening each other. The man you described to Mr. Green is named Peter Macklin. He's a professional working for the woman you eliminated. That wasn't very intelligent of you, Mr. Blossom. These petty personal vendettas are messy and in the long run extremely costly. Frankly, I'm not sure you're useful enough to justify the expense."

"You hang me out to dry I'll open my mouth wide, fucker."

"A response like that is hardly calculated to win my cooperation, Mr. Blossom," said the other, after a pause.

"Yeah, well, hang on to a quarter for tomorrow's *Free Press.*"

"The Macklin situation is being attended to. We have a good man on it. I suggest you proceed as if nothing has happened. Go home, watch television, go to bed. Get up in the morning and go to work."

"Sure, wake up with my brains plastered to the headboard. Jerk off, Brown."

"I've said the situation is in hand. We know far more about this man Macklin than you and he is too cautious to risk coming back tonight. But just in case he does, we have that end covered. It's important that you behave normally. The police are watching you."

The information startled him. "How come?"

"Don't be alarmed. It's Macklin they're after. But we can't afford your attracting their attention."

"They ask me what happened I tell them what, my interior decorator uses double-o buck?"

"Tell them nothing. You were out to dinner, and when you returned you found your apartment a shambles and the police on the premises. They won't believe you, but they won't press the matter. Macklin's the one they want."

Blossom remained silent while a pair of businessmen who had just entered the restaurant removed their overcoats and hung them on the tree next to the telephone. After they moved away: "You better hope what you're telling me sticks, Brown. I'm down in the books as whacked out. Even if I go away for Moira, I'm out of the hatch in two years tops. Then I come looking."

Hanging up, he heard a faint squealing, the gnashing of tiny teeth.

•   •   •

Floyd Arthur had the old man down as a teaching fellow, one of these Old World types who had grown tired of waiting for their accreditation to catch up with them and resigned themselves to assistant professorships in departments too broad for their specialties. He had that slightly seedy look, a topcoat too light for the November-like weather and a silly hat and those round-lensed bifocals you couldn't get here, reflecting the light flatly as he looked around on his way up to the counter—that studied, unfashionable academic conceit fading into bored complacency. He used to see them often in his little chemist's shop off the University of Detroit campus before the new breed of post-Watergate liberals came in wearing their blown hair and windowpane jackets over turtlenecks and shoved them aside. He missed them.

"Yes, sir," Arthur said brightly, leaning on his palms on the countertop.

"I did not expect you still to be open when I called," returned the old man. His voice was heavily accented, with a slightly British inflection. He had learned his English overseas.

"I get most of my business after classes are out. I open in the morning for two hours at seven and then close until noon. You asked about mercury."

"Yes, I need it for a classroom demonstration."

"I don't get much call for it anymore, after all the bad publicity. I'll have to see your faculty card. Some proof you're authorized to handle it."

The old man produced a decaying wallet from his hip pocket and selected a blue-and-yellow card from a thick bundle of them in the photograph section. It was smudged and dog-eared, the lettering barely legible. Arthur accepted it. "Oh, you're with the U of M. I thought you were local."

"No. I filed a requisition with the university, but the shipment hasn't come in and I need the mercury tomorrow. None of the shops in Ann Arbor carries it."

The chemist returned the card, unlocked a cabinet behind the counter, and took down a half-pint plastic bottle from the top shelf. It was much heavier than its size indicated.

"It's fascinating stuff," he said, squinting at the price code on the label. "When I was in eighth grade science, we used to sneak into the room during lunch hour and play with it, chase the little drops around a desktop with our fingers. We didn't know it was poisonous then. I guess that's why none of us got sick. That's twenty-six dollars with the tax."

"Yes, it is deadly." The old man counted two tens, a five, and a single out of his wallet.

Arthur rang it up on the register, slipped the bottle and the receipt into a paper bag, and held it out. "Thanks for coming in, Dr. Wanze," he said.

"Thank you."

Chapter Thirty-two

Morning glowered sullenly through a thin sheeting of dirty white cloud, graying out the skyline to the east and flattening perspectives so that the entire city looked like a dusty board game turned on end. Entering suburban Melvindale, Macklin told his cabdriver to slow down as they passed the entrance to the subterranean salt mines. From the street he could see only the outbuildings and part of the well-marked opening of the shaft and men in yellow hard hats and caked coveralls moving around in front. The cab passed within inches of a plain gray Chevrolet parked across from the entrance with two men in the front seat. Raising his hand on that side as if to scratch his temple, Macklin directed the driver to keep going.

After leaving Roy Blossom's duplex the killer had caught a late supper in a diner, then returned to his motel room to sleep the rest of the night. He had been jumpy after the debacle, angry with himself for his lack of caution, but he had ceased thinking about it the minute he hit the sheets. A lifetime of conditioning and the legacy of a father who had worked years of double shifts as a junkman and truck dispatcher (and weekends cracking skulls for pin money) had given him the ability to sleep anywhere without fanfare. He had risen with the sun, cleaned and oiled his pistol, brushed his clothes and dressed with all the elaborate attention to detail of a matador preparing for the bullring. After that he had gone straight to a cab stand without stopping for breakfast.

Three blocks beyond the mine entrance he told the driver to pull over and paid him and got out. He kept walking in the direction they had been going while the cab was in sight, then reversed himself as it turned the corner and made his way back. The cold air chapped his hands and made an ice mask of his face, but the synthetic material of the sport coat trapped his body heat. Adrenaline crackled through his veins.

A bar with a red Budweiser sign in the window stood in the middle of the last block before the mine. Macklin pushed through the glass door, blinked in the dim interior lighting, and took a stool at the bar, behind which mirrors plated the wall in back of the bottles. At that hour he shared the bar with only two other customers, large men approaching middle age and seated together at a back booth. They wore rough gray coveralls salted white in the creases.

While Macklin was watching them in the mirrors, a stout waitress in her fifties with a beehive of hair dyed bright copper trundled up to their table and set a pair of foaming glasses in front of them. "Salt in your beer, Ed?" she asked.

"That's funny, Arlene. I ain't heard that one all week." The older of the two, a graying giant with an old forked scar on one leathery cheek, excavated a crushed bill from the breast pocket of his coveralls and paid for the beers.

"What's yours?"

Macklin looked up at a freckled bartender in a green T-shirt and dog tags standing behind the bar. "Coke."

After paying for it he sipped it slowly, pretending to listen to the call-in program droning out of the radio over the beer taps. A woman with a Little Rock drawl was asking the guest, a writer, where he got his ideas. The writer said, "Cheboygan."

Ed's companion finished his beer first and got up to leave. Ed rose too, and they shook hands. With a little wave to the waitress the other man left, after which his friend sat down and drank the rest of his beer. He stood again finally, laid two quarters on the table for a tip, and went back toward the rest rooms. Macklin drained his glass unhurriedly and followed.

Ed was standing at the gang urinal, a long tub with black iron starting to show through the white enamel. He glanced up at the mirror in front of him as Macklin entered, nodded a greeting, then shook off and zipped up his fly. Passing behind him, Macklin jerked his right arm up stiffly, driving the heel of his hand into the back of the man's head. Ed's forehead struck the mirror hard, shooting spidery cracks out from the point of impact. He grunted, his forehead bleeding, but before he could move Macklin bounced the edge of the same hand off the big muscle on the side of Ed's neck and his knees buckled. The killer caught him as he fell, lowering him to the floor gently.

Working swiftly, Macklin got the big man's coveralls off and stepped into them. They were big enough to fit into without taking off his sport coat, but he did so anyway, to keep the sleeves from binding, and turned back the cuffs on the coveralls sleeves and pants legs. He looked at his bee-eyed reflection in the broken mirror. It was a loose fit but not enough to attract attention. He took a moment to turn out the sport coat's pockets for forgotten evidence, then dropped it to the floor beside Ed's unconscious form. He was a lousy tipper anyway.

The room's only ventilation came through an amber pebbled-glass window tilting inward at a forty-five-degree angle to its frame. He yanked it horizontal, braced his hands on the sill, and wriggled his head and shoulders through the space underneath. Cold air touched him. He knew an instant of fear when the loosely bunched material around his hips caught, but he pushed hard and came free and got one leg outside and braced himself and freed his other leg and hopped four feet to the pavement. He was in an alley

between the bar and the blank wall of an appliance warehouse next door.

The street behind the bar dead-ended at the cyclone fence
surrounding the entrance to the mine, with another alley
leading to the street that ran in front. Macklin came out there
and walked through the open gate without turning to look at
the men in the car parked across the way. A bored security
guard in a padded jacket with a pile collar barely glanced at
him as he passed in his coveralls. He kept walking.

"Hey!"

Ignoring the shout behind him, he stepped up his pace.
His hand went into his right slash pocket, where he had
placed the 10-millimeter for easy access.

"You! Wait up!"

The calls were drawing attention from the workers milling
around him. He turned, his hand closing around the pistol. A
bearded party with FOREMAN stenciled across the front of his
safety helmet strode up on him.

"Put on a hard hat, you stupid son of a bitch," he said.
"You want the company's insurance yanked?"

Macklin took his hand out of the pocket empty. "I forgot."

"Well?"

The killer left him to select one of the yellow helmets from
the bench the foreman had indicated. It was cold to the
touch and felt clammy on his head. When he turned, the
foreman was still there watching him. "What's your name?"

He hesitated a beat. "Martin."

"Martin."

Macklin watched him scratching his beard.

"You look a little light-skinned for the Martin I know," the
foreman said. "You got a first name?"

"Ed."

He scratched some more. "You from nightside?"

"I just changed shifts."

"Okay. Watch that safety equipment, Martin. We had two
warnings this month already."

Macklin said he would.

The entrance was a cavern shored with creosoted timber and strung with electric bulbs in steel cages. Hills of salt so white it hurt to look at them surrounded the clearing outside, where the rumble of heavy trucks backing up to load made the ground tingle beneath Macklin's feet. He stepped inside, avoiding the narrow-gauge tracks used by the loading cars. The air inside was ten degrees cooler and so dry it seemed to suck the moisture right out of his skin.

Thirty yards in, the main tunnel branched into three separate shafts, fanning out from the center like the spokes of a broken wheel. There would be other levels, more shafts. Finding Blossom in the maze could be one for Jason.

He was turning it over when a black man in hard hat and coveralls came out of the shaft to his left, peeling off a pair of yellow chamois gloves crusted over white.

"Foreman wants to talk to Roy Blossom," he told the newcomer. "You seen him?"

The black man looked at him. "What's the matter with the radio?"

Shit, he hadn't even known they *had* radios. The APB had caused him to force things at the sacrifice of his homework. "No one's answering."

"Fucking things never do work in here. Try C. He rotated out of my corridor last week."

When Macklin didn't move, the black man made a snicking sound with his lips against his teeth and pointed down the shaft across the way. "How long you been here?"

"This is my first day."

"You better leave a trail of bread crumbs. You get turned around down there somebody sprinkles your bones in his soup a hundred years from tomorrow."

He started down the shaft indicated. It was narrower than the main corridor, and once he had to flatten out against the rock wall while a line of cars clattered past loaded with chunks of salt and towed by an electric engine with a hard hat at the controls. The ground declined at a gentle but steady angle. Although his sense of distance and direction had stayed behind on the surface, he knew with an icy clutch of claustrophobia when he had passed beneath the Detroit River. He was in a dead womb with millions of gallons of water pressing down from above.

He walked for what seemed miles without meeting anyone. Then he rounded a bend and found himself in a broad section filled with men standing in three feet of snow.

Under the vapor of spent breath twisting toward the humming ventilator ducts overhead, snow hardly seemed out of place. But he was looking at boulder-size chunks of crystallized salt that had been jarred loose from the white walls. In that ghost-lit cavern colonnaded with saline pillars as thick as tree trunks, the men loading the pieces by hand into a train of ore cars looked like trolls at work in a fairy castle of ice.

He broke out of his trance finally and joined them, bending to help scoop pieces into the cars. They were sandpapery to the touch and much lighter than their size indicated. After a few minutes his palms began to feel incredibly dry, almost brittle. He paused to pat his pockets, found a pair of chamois gloves on his left hip, and wriggled his fingers into them, studying the faces of the men around him as he adjusted the gauntlets over his cuffs. But in the harsh electric light the peaks of their hard hats threw their faces into shadow, and he looked in vain for the arrogant features he had memorized. He resumed working.

A chunk hurled with too much enthusiasm skipped off the mound in the last car, brushing the shoulder of a man working on the other side. "Hey!"

The man who had thrown it shrugged. "Sorry."

"You do it again you will be."

Macklin watched the man who had been brushed swagger over to lift the errant piece and flip it into the car. He recognized the gait, the angle of the head. Slowly he worked his way toward him.

They loaded side by side for some minutes, Blossom never turning his head to look at the man nearest him. Finally one of the hard hats told the others to stand away and took his place at the controls of the electric engine. The little train started with a splatter of sparks and rolled away up the tunnel, picking up speed as it went.

"Clear!"

Blossom and the others backed toward the right wall. Macklin followed their lead. The worker who had shouted gripped the sling handle of a pneumatic drill built along the lines of a machine gun on a tripod and elevated the bit. Macklin managed to get his fingers in his ears just as the man pressed the trigger. The rattle-bang was deafening in the enclosed space. Cracks spidered out along the jagged white wall and pieces dropped loose as from a jigsaw puzzle, raining down silently under the din and raising a cloud of grainy white dust that powdered hard hats and coveralls and parched Macklin's nostrils as he breathed in spite of himself.

Some of the others had their fingers in their ears, but most did not. He suspected they were wearing earplugs and he searched the pockets of Ed's coveralls for a pair but found none. Well, if all the explosions he'd been in lately hadn't thickened his eardrums, nothing would.

A narrower shaft opened to his right, not as brightly lit as this one. Macklin glanced around, saw that the others were busy watching the drilling, and shoved his pistol into Roy Blossom's ribs. He gave him time to react and to recognize him, then nodded toward the opening. After a moment the other turned that way. Macklin followed with the gun at kidney level. Behind them the drill clattered.

Chapter Thirty-three

The door opened the width of the man standing inside, which was not wide enough to allow Burlingame a look at the room behind him. A faint odor of floor wax and vintage sweat skirled out, gymnasium smells.

"Mr. Anderson?" said Burlingame.

"My name's Green. Who are you?" But the look on the narrow man's face, bracketed by sideburns that reached to the angles of his jaw, told the FBI man he had been recognized. The man had on an orange necktie bright enough to stop a train.

"Green's good. Your CIA jacket says you're not much for exotic aliases. Kurof in?"

"There's no Kurof here." The door started to close. Burlingame blocked it with a shoulder and waved his ID.

"Official business, friend. I can get a warrant, but we're brothers in red, white, and blue. We shouldn't have to do that sort of thing."

"Open the door, Mr. Green."

"Green" started a little at the deep tones behind him, then backed away, bringing the door in with him.

Burlingame entered. With the light streaming in through the pebbled glass high in the far wall, the man standing in the center of the glossy blond-oak floor was a shadowy bulk with gray in his thick hair, built like a refrigerator.

The FBI man said, "I wondered for a long time why a

gymnasium. Then I went back to your file. Rome, 1956. Wrestling and hammer-throwing. You took a bronze medal."

"Nostalgia, Mr. Burlingame," said the man in shadow. "It grows as our balls wither."

"Speak for yourself."

The other opened his mouth and laughed, a peasant's roar. "I'm glad we met," he said when it was over. "So many Americans in your work are too serious. They don't understand the beauty of the game, only its end."

"They like clear sides. The crowned checkers that move both ways just confuse them. Not me. When you've been playing it this long you get to welcome the double reverse. Keeps you awake. Anderson was a nice surprise."

"Mr. Green is here to see I don't take pictures of secret installations before my asylum comes through."

"Bullshit. He's got eight years in liaison. He doesn't baby-sit suspected spies."

"How do you know that?" barked the narrow man.

"Office secret. Like Kurof's relationship with the CIA."

"Brown, please," said the man in shadow. "I've grown used to it. I'm thinking of making it legal when I become a citizen. What cards are you holding, Mr. Burlingame?"

"Don't worry, I'm not wired. Anderson can check me. Or does he prefer Green?"

Brown moved a massive shoulder. Green directed the FBI man to raise his hands, then spread his coat and patted him down. He removed Burlingame's revolver and stuck it in his waistband.

Lowering his arms, Burlingame said: "I considered the possibility of Green's being a rogue agent, but there were too many people watching you for that. Then we got a court order to pull Roy Blossom's file at the Ypsilanti mental hospital. He had only one visitor his whole stay. The description fit you."

"My build and coloring are not unique," said Brown.

"I know you're working for the Company. Green here is

your go-between. I know you've got something going with Blossom and that it's heavy enough to hire three different killers to try to take out Peter Macklin when he accepted a contract to kill him. It's details I'm after."

"To what purpose? Even if you're right about me, the FBI and the CIA work for the same employer."

"Our paychecks come in the same kind of envelope. After that it's a big scramble for appropriations from Congress and the loser gets to go home sucking his wounds. I figure between the two of us we're spending a couple of billion a year listening at each other's keyholes. I'm not out to kick over any pots, though. I'm just trying to keep peace in my jurisdiction. If I can leave here with some assurance that this thing isn't going to stretch into my next pay period I'll be happy as a pig with its own tit. And some answers."

"That's what you want. What are you bargaining?"

"The Bureau backs off from this one, hands in the air."

"That's all?"

"It's more than my late great boss would have promised, and you won't hear it again from my office. Provided I like what I hear."

"Close the door, please, Mr. Green."

After a moment Green complied. Brown turned and Burlingame followed him deeper into the echoing room. With the change of angle he got a better look at his host, his cod-colored eyes, the blue shadow covering the lower half of his face. He had seen him before only in photographs. Brown stopped under a slanting shaft of light.

"You'll do nothing with the information," he said. "In return for my promise that the business stops today, win or lose, without loss to the Bureau or innocent parties."

"Jesus," said Green, "you're not asking him for his *word*?"

Burlingame ignored him. "No more bodies?"

"One more."

"Macklin's?"

Brown shrugged.

"I need answers," Burlingame said. "The local police are in it and I don't much like being the guy who takes the heat for committing an entire detail of field agents to dog another U.S. operative for eleven months. I'd like retirement to be my idea. So let's roll."

"That is the other thing, the police. I have no wish to deal with them."

"Everyone thinks I have influence with the police but the police. There's an inspector working this one who reminds me of me. But I'll do what I can."

"I trust you. I think we're much alike."

"Bite your tongue, you overdressed Communist."

"I am not overdressed." Brown laughed again. "*Citizen Kane.* It plays in the U.S.S.R. as a chronicle of American decadence." He sobered. "The CIA is a stalking horse. Behind it is another organization, smaller and quieter, but referred to by a name so long I sometimes forget it myself. I've worked for and with it on and off for sixteen years."

"I know the one. Clerks and auditors."

"The material collected and codified by those clerks and auditors would reveal Watergate as one small part of a master plan. But that's too complex to go into and frankly it bores me. Anyway, after my assignment here, I was placed in charge of the international border in this region. Oh, not the check posts, which are well patrolled by the Customs officials of both countries. My jurisdiction covers the little holes no one thinks about. Wyandotte, where it's a ten-minute swim to Windsor. Boblo Island, in the middle of the river, between Detroit and Amherstburg. I watched with interest your negotiations with those tour-boat hijackers last August, but when they sailed into Lake Erie and out of my charge I stayed clear. That was when I first heard of this man Macklin, and why I decided not to waltz with him now. The international salt mines beneath the river."

"Blossom. He works in the mines."

"I transferred him there after his release from Ypsilanti.

He had the aptitude as a former coal miner in Pennsylvania. Before that my predecessor had him working deep cover in the local pornography industry. Those film cans carry a lot of cocaine and heroin and one of his duties was to monitor the traffic. He is a close observer and his memory for details is phenomenal. His kind is rare."

"Glad to hear it. He's a psycho."

"That embarrassment is secondary. His insanity defense was laid by a specialist attorney hired through a government cover. So long as they remain useful we stand behind our own."

"What's he doing in the mines?"

"That's one question you don't get to ask. It's enough to know those mines are a weak spot in the nation's security."

"How's a former Politburo hopeful get to stand on the U.S. border?"

"Ah"—showing his teeth now—"the double double reverse. A one-man Temple Guard is a temptation to assassins if they can but identify him. Who'd suspect a suspected double agent under the surveillance of the CIA and the FBI?"

"That's Washington," Burlingame said after a moment. "Never go directly from A to B with X so close. But there's more to it than that."

"Probably. But I go where they tell me. I'm too old to look for another job. And I like this one."

"Blossom's no sentinel. Psychopathic killers stashed in the exits are to keep people in, not out. Is that the new line in national security, scorched earth?"

Brown laid a thick finger beside his nose.

"Fixed nuclear warheads placed at strategic sites across the country are among the worst-kept secrets in Washington. They aren't there to blow up the enemy."

"Jesus."

"Exactly. The model for the plan."

"Self-crucifixion wasn't His way."

"Nor is it ours. This is just a layman's hypothesis constructed on known evidence. We don't know why those warheads are there."

"But you know why Blossom's in the mines."

"Yes, but that isn't part of our bargain."

Burlingame paused. The huge room felt cool with just the three standing in the center, Green off from the others a little, studying his reflection smeared across the varnished floor. A criminal waste of space in an overcrowded world. "It ends today."

"I've promised that." Brown extended a large hand.

The FBI man didn't move. "My job says I have to make deals with people who hire killers to protect other killers. What I do with my hands is personal."

Brown lowered his. "I'm sorry we can't be friends."

"Like hell you are."

Outside, Burlingame breathed cold air and sweet-sour auto exhaust. That night was Devil's Night, to be followed by Halloween and then November and then the long bitter slide into winter, his last with the Bureau. He didn't know until he looked down at his hands that he was holding his pipe. He snapped it in two and hurled the pieces to the sidewalk before moving on.

All the killers weren't on the streets.

Chapter Thirty-four

Dry cold. A man left dead in that narrow white tunnel would never decay, his flesh preserved like the eighty-year-old mining equipment by salt and the unchanging forty-two-degree temperature. The two men walked single-file down the passage for three hundred yards and met no one. The pneumatic drill rapped on like firecrackers in a bottle. Then it stopped.

Macklin called for Blossom to hold up. In the sudden silence on the end of the noise the monosyllabic command rang and rang in the tunnel. The miner obeyed, keeping his hands away from his body as ordered. Oxygen hummed out of the ventilators.

Macklin waited. In his desire to get as far away from the other miners as possible he had taken too long, and now he would have to wait until the drilling resumed. In a public place he would have fired and counted on the noise of the report to frighten off the heroes. But down here, in this masculine mélange, among the Brotherhood of the Subterranean, the rules were different. A shot would bring the others running. They would overpower and disarm him and if they didn't tear him apart right there they would hold him for the police. He waited.

"Hey, guy?" Blossom's head was turned slightly. Macklin could see the bone structure of his forehead and left cheek under the peak of his helmet.

"Shut up."

"I didn't do Moira. It was one of them dopers. It's a wrong neighborhood."

Macklin said nothing.

"Hey, I liked her too. Maybe you and me can work together, get the fuckers that did her, what do you say?"

"Shut up."

Blossom was silent for a little. Then: "Hey, guy? I know what you're waiting for. It ain't going to work. This here tunnel's a shortcut to the outside. Somebody'll come along using it any minute. You got another hour to wait before that drill starts up again. What you going to do, shoot whoever comes along?"

Macklin told him a third time to shut up. He saw only waste in conversing with the dead.

"Let's have the knife," he said after a minute.

Pause. "I ain't—"

He took two steps and laid the 10-millimeter's barrel across Blossom's exposed temple. The miner's hard hat tumbled off and he sagged against the rough wall. Macklin ran a hand into the stricken man's right slash pocket and came out holding a heavy clasp knife.

"Don't cut me," Blossom whimpered. He was supporting himself against the wall.

"That what Moira said?" Macklin brought the gun down butt first on the other's collarbone. The miner howled and slid the rest of the way into a sitting position on the floor of the shaft. He was blubbering now.

"I didn't do her."

"You piece of shit." The killer planted the sole of a shoe high on Blossom's back and shoved him sprawling onto his face.

"So much emotion."

He fought the urge to spin around at the sound of the new voice behind him. Instead he turned slowly, pocketing the miner's knife in the same movement.

"Gun."

It was the way he said it. Macklin let go of the pistol instantly. It clattered to the salt floor. He looked at a pudgy man in his late fifties or early sixties wearing a topcoat over a green sweater and a hard hat too large for him that rested on top of his round bifocals. His arm was extended level with his shoulder and ended in a lean semiautomatic pistol with a bore no bigger around than a man's little finger.

As Macklin remained standing with his hands away from his sides, the pistol came down to rest on the newcomer's hipbone. It was a Walther.

"I guess that makes you Mantis," Macklin said.

The little round man wrinkled his nose. "Signs and countersigns, code names and passwords. It is all like small boys playing at pirates. Novo is good enough; in fact, preferred."

"How'd you get in here?"

He cocked his head toward a laminated card dangling from a clothespin on his lapel. "Inspector. The same man who got Mr. Blossom his job found employment for me also." He pushed back his hard hat with his free hand and let it fall. From the bulging pocket of his coat he pulled a squashed hat and slapped it against his thigh and hooked it on over the back of his balding head. Macklin recognized the feather in the band.

"Those exploding bullets are more trouble than they're worth," he said.

"These are quite effective, and since the pieces left are too small to preserve striations, I can use the same weapon several times without detection. This time, however, I had to replace it. You were dead, I threw it away. But you were not as dead as I like."

"You had me at my place in the country. The fuse was a second too long. In Taylor you didn't even come close. By then I had your pattern. Not this time, though. This time I was stupid."

Novo said, "It is the main paradox of our work. Habits are fatal and so we avoid them. But for every killer there is one perfect method and so we make it a habit, thereby inviting disaster while seeking success. Mr. Blossom was yours. Where he is, there are you."

"Don't pop him too quick."

Novo's eyes flicked behind Macklin. Macklin could hear the scraping sounds of Blossom getting to his feet. Out of the corner of his eye he saw one of the miner's slender hands lifting the 10-millimeter from the floor. He started to turn that way. Novo's gun twitched and he stopped.

"I'm going to bang you up good," Blossom said behind Macklin. "Then I'm going to carve on you, just like Moira. There's lots better things to cut off on you."

The Walther's muzzle flashed. Macklin heard the nasty, popping report and flinched, his stomach muscles tightening for the impact.

Behind him Blossom whimpered.

Into the long silence on the end of the echo, laundry fell. Something heavy nudged the back of Macklin's legs. He heard the breath leaving Blossom's body in a long sigh.

He screwed up his brow at the Bulgarian.

"An embarrassment," said Novo. "Mr. Blossom had his uses to a point. After that he became . . ." He groped for the word.

Macklin said, "A liability."

"An expense. My employer chose to cut his losses. You stopped being the target last night, when some indiscreet person murdered a mirror in Mr. Blossom's apartment and involved yet another branch of the police." His cherubic face exaggerated innocence. "Things are so complicated here. Where I come from there is only one authority to be concerned about."

"The contract is canceled."

"Contract? Oh, yes, your former employers' colorful word for it. Yes, it has been withdrawn."

"You knew Moira King was going to hire me to kill Blossom before I ever heard of any of them. How?"

"My employers ran surveillance on all of her acquaintances. Your first call to Howard Klegg on another matter was recorded off a tap on his wire. Following a background check on you, the rather crude gentleman with the flamethrower was placed on alert. Your conversation in Klegg's office, overheard through means which are beyond my poor peasant's understanding, confirmed their worst fears and he was ordered into position."

"Simple."

"Yet complex."

"We're done then, you and I?" Macklin rested his hands in his pockets.

"I think we are not." The round glasses had slipped a little, reflecting light in two blank circles. "My dead mother had a theory about weeds in the garden," he said. "It was not enough that they be uprooted, for she believed that the roots would re-anchor themselves and the weeds would grow back. They must be burned, the ashes buried far from the garden. Otherwise they will have to be uprooted again and maybe not in time to save the tomatoes."

"You're not a weed?"

"I have no such illusion. A weed does not say to itself, wait, look here, perhaps this is a brother weed I am choking. He strangles all obstacles in the path of his growth. We can learn much from our cousins the weeds. A killer left alive can only turn up somewhere else. Where two exist there can be no truce."

"The shot," Macklin said.

"By now the others have blamed it on a falling rock. I will not be here when they come to investigate the second. This tunnel is an exit. Give me your interesting weapon, Mr. Macklin. It is behind your left foot."

It had slid out of Blossom's hand when he fell. Macklin rescued it from the blood and viscera of the miner's exploded face and stepped forward to hand it to Novo.

"With one of these bullets in your body and the proper

guns left in the proper dead hands the police will leap to the most convenient conclusion," said the other, accepting it. "My mother had a most successful garden, by the way. Everyone said so."

The drill started up again at the other end of the shaft, racketing like a machine gun. Blossom had lied about that too. Following through on his forward movement, Macklin tore his hand out of the pocket of his coveralls and arched it up under the swell of Novo's paunch.

He felt the old man gasp, blood running hot over the blade of the open clasp knife, and wrenched it sideways, sensing weight on his arm, things spilling out. At the same time he plucked the Walther out of Novo's weakening grasp and stepped back quickly. The Bulgarian knelt with his hands clasped under his belly like a pregnant woman praying.

He had not yet fallen when Macklin finished smearing his fingerprints on the gun and knife and flipped them in the general direction of their respective owners. Last he picked up the 10-millimeter from where it had dropped for the third time. By then Novo had flopped over onto his side, drawing his knees up into a fetal curl.

The drilling was very loud and Macklin had to shout to be heard by the dying man.

"You talk too much."

He went out the short way, secreting the gun and his bloodstained hand in a pocket.

Chapter Thirty-five

His apartment complex in Southfield looked smaller, like a childhood home revisited. He paid his driver and went in through the front door. It felt good to use his own key.

The foyer felt warm. The air outside was metal cold, and the weatherman was predicting snow for Halloween. He was in his shirtsleeves, having discarded the coveralls in a city dumpster; the hard hat had been checked at the mine and the 10-millimeter pistol was well on its way to Lake Erie by way of the Detroit sewer system.

He had made his way past the guard and miners lounging on a break outside the mine exit without being stopped. The occupants of a second unmarked car parked across the street from that gate had appeared to show some interest in him as he emerged, but then a DSR bus had whooshed to a stop in front of him and he boarded. The car hadn't followed. Everyone knew professional killers didn't use public transportation.

A twinge of precognition tingled under his skin on the staircase to his floor. He ignored it as left over from the stairwell of Howard Klegg's building and continued to his corner apartment.

Inside, among familiar things, he felt strange. He'd grown used to the impersonal surrounding of rented rooms. His own slightly worn furniture, the odd items of clothing draped over the chairs and sofa and hanging from the top of the open bedroom door embarrassed him somehow, as if he'd been shown a nude picture of himself. Anonymity was the killer's watchword and he felt most vulnerable among his own possessions. He wondered if there was a clinical term for the fear of the known.

He was still tingling. Something, what was it? He sniffed the air. It was too fresh. Not stale at all after having been closed in for more than a week. And in the realization he turned back toward the door.

But it opened as he was reaching for the knob, and Sergeant Lovelady's wrinkled yellow sport coat filled the doorway. He was holding a Police Special, above which his pale dented face gave up no more expression than a whitewashed fence.

"Just so it's legal." Inspector Pontier, tall and black and slender and bald, came in from the bedroom holding out a long fold of white paper with an official-looking border. "Your landlord let us in."

Macklin didn't accept the paper. "I guess it's legal if you've got it."

"Position," said Lovelady.

Macklin leaned on his palms on the wall next to the door and let the fat sergeant kick his feet apart and grope him from neck to ankles.

Lovelady stepped back. "Clean, Inspector."

"Why aren't I surprised."

Macklin pushed away from the wall and turned around, lowering his hands. The door was closed now and the sergeant's gun was out of sight. Pontier said, "I hope you don't mind. I've been using your telephone to monitor things in Melvindale. They wanted me there on the spot but when I found out neither of those bodies was yours we made ourselves comfortable here. You're never around by the time the corpses turn up."

"I'm not following any of this, of course. I haven't been to Melvindale in months."

The inspector's gray eyes were fixed planets in his face.

"You're good. I never said you weren't. Burlingame filled me in on this guy Mantis, and you can't ever predict what a giggler like Blossom is going to do next."

Macklin made no response. He felt Lovelady watching him from his corner.

"You were seen entering and leaving the mine," Pontier said. "I don't have any reports on that yet but I will. Any one of those officers will pick you out of a lineup."

"Say they do. What's the penalty for impersonating a miner?"

"Who said you impersonated a miner?"

"Not me," said Macklin.

The inspector's amiable expression shut down hard. "I don't like cute, Macklin. I don't even have to fuck around with charges. I can have Sergeant Lovelady blow off your face and plant a throwaway piece on you and claim self-defense. You ought to know how that works. You doctored the evidence at the mine pretty good."

"Lovelady never killed anyone."

"I knew it," the sergeant said.

"Shut up." To Macklin: "He does what I tell him. Don't think I'm all that straight, fucker. Even a straight cop gets tired of watching killers squirt through his fingers. I could blast you and sleep like a nun."

The killer uncoiled a little. He'd been afraid Pontier had something. "I'm tired, Inspector. I was up early. Do I sleep here or downtown?"

"Cuff him."

The sergeant hurled him back up against the wall hard, hooked a handcuff on his right wrist, yanked it down behind his back, did the same with the left, and levered on its mate. He ratcheted them tight.

"You're busted," Pontier said. "For the murder of Moira King."

Macklin faced him. The bracelets were cutting off his circulation. "What's your evidence?"

"Your prints are all over her apartment. We've got a witness who will testify to your relationship."

"This witness wouldn't be Howard Klegg."

"Should it be?"

He said nothing. The inspector looked too eager. Klegg wouldn't testify. He'd have to admit on the witness stand that he'd recommended the killer to her. Which would result in a charge against the lawyer of conspiracy to commit murder.

"What's my motive?"

"Lovers' quarrel, maybe. From what we found out about her she was vulnerable enough for you to be plowing her."

"I was out of town when she was killed." Getting shot at by the Bulgarian.

"Your car was. Got any witnesses to prove you were with it?"

"You know it wasn't me."

"We can hold you on it for now, and when that runs out we'll ring in resisting arrest and assaulting an officer from last night in Melvindale. We're dusting that shotgun you left behind for prints, but Connely and Petersen will ID you anyway. Then the Taylor Police will want to talk to you about a triple murder and arson there yesterday. You got a prime civics lesson coming."

"I've had it before. There isn't anything you can do to me that hasn't been done."

"How about this?" He slammed a balled fist into the pit of Macklin's stomach.

"Jesus," said Lovelady.

The killer jackknifed, bile climbing his throat. His vision clouded and his breathing came in short, shallow sips that burned his lungs. The wave of nausea and pain curled and broke and receded. His senses came swimming back with the tide.

"You and Blossom and this Mantis character have been playing Dungeons and Dragons with my city for a week."

Pontier spoke through his teeth. "I don't give a shit what kind of deal you've got cooking with the feds, they're just visitors here. It's my city, mine. Next time you lay out the pieces, you forget who owns the board, I throw you back in the box you came in and nail down the lid. That clear enough or you want me to repeat it?" He cocked his fist.

"It's clear." Macklin's breath still creaked.

"You better hope it is. You better hope."

Lovelady started to read him his rights.

"Forget that," Pontier said. "Spring him."

The sergeant hesitated. "He ain't busted?"

"I've got a seventy-percent record for arrests that stick. I'm not fucking it up with any heavyweight scum this month."

"What about Connely and Petersen?"

"Let them swear out their own complaint. Somehow I don't think they will. It means admitting they left their post to goon a fender-bender down the block. Come on, the air stinks in here."

"The deputy chief won't like it." The sergeant produced his key and unlocked the cuffs.

"The deputy chief's a prick."

Macklin rubbed his wrists, watching Pontier do up his necktie. "I'm clear?"

"You'll never be that. Not in my city. You want advice? Move. Because no part of the wheel stays out of the shit all the time and when you go under I'm going to be right there standing on the brake."

"I haven't known what's been going on since this one started. If it means anything."

"Not to me. Let's go, Sergeant."

"Aren't you going to read me that speech about not leaving town?"

"Why?" The inspector was at the door, held open by Lovelady. "Blossom stabbed Mantis, and Mantis shot Blossom. That's what the officers on the scene say it looks like and I don't guess the coroner will find anything that says different. Anyway, it's the feds' red wagon, as Burlingame would put it. They'll type it up with a new ribbon for one of their gray cardboard folders and when it goes in the drawer it'll be deader than Sacco and Vanzetti. The feds are a lot like you, Macklin. They clean up after themselves. We finished dusting that shotgun, by the way. There weren't any liftable prints on it. But I guess you knew that."

"I hear you, Inspector. I don't know what you're saying."

Pontier shocked him by making a shrill, screeching noise off the roof of his mouth.

"That's me setting the brake."

He went out. Lovelady followed, closing the door behind them.

Macklin turned the lock. Routinely he walked through the apartment, checking the bedroom and bath for leftover officers, then drew the curtains over the living room windows. After turning on a light he broke his cash out of its hiding place and counted the bills. They were all there. He put them back and went into the kitchen to fix himself a drink.

Taken on an empty stomach, the raw bourbon made his head sing. He wasn't hungry. He could still feel Pontier's fist in his belly.

The telephone rang while he was taking off his shoes in the bedroom. He let it ring and stretched out fully clothed atop the covers. He didn't feel tired but he wanted to sleep. If he stayed awake with no more policemen to talk to or drinks to make, he would start thinking, asking himself questions he couldn't answer. Which in his business was a mistake.

The telephone rang and rang. Twenty-five. Twenty-six. He got up and padded back into the living room and lifted the receiver.

"Macklin?"

"Who's this?"

"Macklin, how the hell are you? It's Charles Maggiore."

He didn't reply. It was Maggiore's voice.

"I hear you've been busy. I tried to reach you earlier but I guess you were out. I wanted to say that's quite a kid you got. Regular peel off the old potato."

"Say it."

"Well, not over the phone. I just wanted to tell you your kid did real good last night. You can be proud."

The line clicked and buzzed. Macklin stood with the receiver to his ear until the recording came on telling him to hang up and dial again. Then he cradled it and checked his watch, turning his wrist to read it in the dim light. Ten to twelve. He went into the kitchen and switched on the radio and poured another drink and waited.

The news came on at noon. The story he was waiting for was tucked between a taped excerpt from the mayor's address to council and a traffic report. At three that morning the body of the owner of a chain of area furniture stores had been found in a dumpster behind one of his buildings with a .22 slug in the back of his head. He had been dead several hours. There were no suspects as yet, but according to the police, the dead man had a record of business dealings with organized crime figures locally. Macklin spun the dial but could catch no other news programs. He turned off the radio.

And he had to find another divorce lawyer.